Alone, with the Good Graces

Thomas F. Sheehan

Pocol Press

Fairfax, VA

POCOL PRESS
Published in the United States of America
by Pocol Press
3911 Prosperity Avenue
Fairfax, VA 22031
www.pocolpress.com

Publisher's Cataloguing-in-Publication

Names: Sheehan, Thomas F., 1928-, author.
Title: Alone , with the good graces / Thomas F. Sheehan.
Description: Fairfax, VA : Pocol Press, 2018.
Identifiers: LCCN 2018966166 | ISBN 978-1-929763-85-6
Subjects: LCSH Short stories, American. | War--Fiction. | Family--Fiction. | Crime--Fiction. | BISAC FICTION / Short Stories (single author)
Classification: LCC PS3569.H39216 A46 2018 | DDC 813.54--dc23

Library of Congress Control Number: 2018966166

ACKNOWLEDGEMENTS

Stories in this volume have appeared in current or earlier versions in the following sites/magazines: *Literally Stories, DM du Jour/Danse Macabre, Orion's Child, Troubadour 21, Mythaxis, Ocean Magazine, NH Pulp Live, Indiana Review, Down in the Dirt, Imitation Fruit, Rope & Wire Western Magazine, Perpetual Magazine, Provo Canyon Review, Green Silk Journal, Belle Reve Literary Journal* and *Tulip Tree.*

TABLE OF CONTENTS

Comes a Prisoner Bound in Rags

The mountains were sunlit, like glory loose of heaven, dark as old souls at their valley roots, in the clutch of earth trembling from a sky-high battle with its last aerial shot not yet fired, its last echo of death riding the sweep of air, when the screeching, not identified, began on high. The sounds of death had breath to spare, and the U.S. Air Force's F86 Sabre pursuit fighter plane from the 4th Fighter Interceptor Wing, out of Suwon Air Base or Kimpo Air Base, both in South Korea, tumbled from the sky, the roar, the screech, the scream of air being sliced nearly by its atoms or other miniscule thinness not measurable by any of the troops facing each other on the ground.

In ghastly sky-shared company, plummeting slower than the aircraft, came its parachuting pilot, free and loose in the air, heading surely to imprisonment, anger, torture, bodily harm, at the hands of North Korean custodians, or Chinese counterparts. The hills below, on both sides of an unmarked battle line, were crowded with troops of several nations, from the very continent, and from countries and other continents across the globe, their new or at least temporary homes being nothing more than holes in the earth, deeply-dug bunkers fortified with logs or sandbags, any place not in direct in-line sighting of small arms fire.

From a hill-top observation post, an army corporal, at the controls of a battery-pack powered SCR-300 radio transceiver (a walkie-talkie), carried for his commanding officer directing the attack of U.S. infantry units, reported to his base headquarters, after some hillside interruptions causing garbled communication: "Please advise Air Force the loss of one F86 Sabre Jet aircraft, just shot down and crashed beyond Hill 598 near Kumhwa, its pilot in parachute deployment now and settling into enemy custody." He added, in a different tone of voice, a soldier of an honest and neutral appreciation, "We have no further information on pilot or plane, but both apparently are goners." He almost swallowed his own words; "Goners, I said, absolute goners!"

Air Force officials, eventually via regular service connections through the War Department and a volunteer at the Post Office, delivered a telegram to the pilot's lone family member, a brother in St. Louis, Missouri. The telegram carried note of his brother, Charles Egert Dawsing, being "missing in action" in Korea. The brother was William Levert Dawsing, senior by six years, a professor with tenure in the English department at St. Louis University.

Professor Dawsing was looked upon by students and fellow instructors as a thoroughly good teacher who used a great deal of drama and emotion in the classroom, and all agreed with a statement his wife had once delivered to a group of cohorts from the university, that "Bill prepares more for his classes than any man I've ever known and we all ought to be thankful for his deep interests at all levels."

She didn't tell anybody that she often heard her husband's words coming through the rooms of their home long after she thought he'd gone to sleep in his study, the way those words rang off walls, stairs, pillars and posts with his orotund voice. Much else of what she did not say, but could have said, considered that she often recognized the words as coming from a famous author or poet in her circle of personal favorites.

Bill Dawsing, the war in Korea in its second or third year, his brother near the end of a year of aerial combat, on one sad and fateful day, saw an old friend coming timorously to his door with a yellow telegram in his hand; he felt the contents before he read the telegram from the War Department.

His mind had searched other grounds in a matter of minutes, not knowing how or where they had originated, or why, inhaled odors savory and unsavory, heard sounds of life ... breaths taken, let go, scuffling feet, knew dust rising and falling back in place, almost detected hands from a hidden tunnel rubbing each other in anticipation of promoting pain, causing harm, threatening the tight little room of life about him from the very second the door swung open.

Then, as often as not, he heard something from beyond the door of the tight little room, a beginning and an ending occurring at the exact same moment, an implausible acceptance of place in the order of things: he was at the point of pain before it arrived in his presence, before it made known unspoken demands, before life began its precarious balance, or played the end of one day against the beginning of another day.

No whisper of things warned him; they were as real as life. Silence, indeed, had something to say; he had long sworn to listen to every sound in the universe that came his way, a peep of a bird, the grunt of a pig, a step on a stairway from utter depths, the hello of the Devil himself.

The sound came once more. He stiffened. It was closer. His whole body knew it was closer, all his parts in concert with each other and the whole being. It was not just in his hearing. It did approach. It did make inroads. It said so. The metal toe. The kick. The slash. Ping Tu smiling through his ugly and malodorous teeth. Oh, would Ping Tu have a thirst for amontillado! Oh, were he himself the finest of stone masons, setting Ping Tu up for the full sentence; to make an end of my labor, to force the last stone into place; to set the best of mortar, forever.

Caught between the professor and the captain!

Again.

In the darkness, in the cell, he had himself convinced for the thousandth time to use all his body parts, to get them all concerted into the game. It was the only way to pass time, evade terrors abounding, to keep a thin shred of sanity if nothing else was there to hold onto. Against darkness he fought and loneliness and the constant threats of bodily harm that came from different directions and at different tempos each day, each hour.

To fight back, he had to hold the final, and internal, control, keep on his toes, to be fully aware of signs and signals of new twists of pain and derision in the offing. Food was a tool both ways; he had to survive with less than they planned to give him, to live on nothing as usual as food, but to look elsewhere for other life.

His torso twisted anew in simple gestures, manipulations and the reach for tools of capture arising again. Thumb and finger. Thumb and finger. He had them poised, ready to clutch, grasp, snare what vermin of his cell dared be caught. If the smallest of the lot trod the ground between those pincers, he'd have an addition to any bit of food. Perhaps the entrée, though small as it promised. In the pit of darkness, this room with no aperture, no stars allowed, no moon, no haze off the unseen horizon, silence baiting him as always, he could not see thumb and finger. But they were there a perilous distance apart. Then for hours, in the absolute darkness, they were but a whisper apart, a hair's breadth, and at times his whole arm trembled from the noble and vowed concentration. The length of that side of his body, at times down to his toes, knew that tremble as a simple arc of electricity, but knew the burn it could threaten.

Now, there was another thing ... the toes. Time after time in the darkness he had tried to master a most difficult manipulation, to squeeze a big toe against its neighbor when he felt the vermin at that extremity, picking or digging its way through or into his skin. Way back in his memory, from an old news film maybe, he could bring back the picture of an old man making baskets; weaving, for god's sake, baskets out of strips of dried grass, with his toes! Toes like fingers! Toes using a double-edged razor blade to strip the grass or reeds into long, slender pieces! A lifetime at it, most likely, and that a likely mental reservation of his own. "I'm due a few," he said aloud in the circumscription of the imposed cell.

Would toes be at a greater advantage for vermin catching, them so unsuspecting? Ha! thinking like that! What an attribute for them! Or then, there was that other older man he remembered, one without arms, who typed with his toes, he too in an old film of sorts that came flying back on demand. Oh, he could see the carriage return sling backwards harsh as a rifle bolt, could hear the bell click on an old L. C. Smith-Corona, a metal monster with music in its own right, the dumb, inert, potential of great novels, short stories cutting to the quick, poems that could melt him down in their abject simplicity. All from that black giant of quick mechanics. He could hear it again and again, that musical bell, that energy sign. Oh, the short sentences of the solitary typist at his task, digging at his brain, punching with his toes. Hemingway stuff, stripped down to the nerves themselves. Adjectives coming alive in the stream. The return bell ringing and ringing. Most likely an A Flat, he'd try to convince himself, though tone deaf. The bull charged. The people ran. Pamplona exploded. A Flat, without a doubt. A Flat. A Flat.

Then the itch, invariably, would begin at a point on his back he could not reach, and it was arriving again by the clock, perfectly timed in its entrance. At the small of the back, as if in between the cruddy vest remnants he wore, forced on him by the prison captain, and the worn and thin blanket he tried to sleep on, infested no doubt with creatures warmer than he'd ever be again. Bare, the air talking on his skin, his arms, at least the one not shivering, felt the chill, knew it to the bone, trying to be company with the itch.

A shiver, a body's full shiver every once in a while, the entire course of him, was the most pleasure he might have for hours. It would attest to his total consciousness, his whole being, as much a passage fully memorized and fully realized from his old reading days taking hold of him, finding his soul, freeing the very words in their simple grandeur, their grand simplicity: It must be understood that neither by word nor deed had I given Fortunato cause to doubt my good will. I continued, as was my wont, to smile in his face, and he did not perceive that my smile now was at the thought of his immolation.

Oh, dear Christ in nearest heaven, he had catapulted now through E.A. Poe to the captain; jailer extraordinary, stick wielder, percussionist, with the long yellow teeth, the sneer and contempt embedded in his face, his all-out hatred in-born for America and the mothers of prisoners and the Grand Canyon and a Saturday full of football and spring loaded with baseballs echoing off the bats. The captain, Ping Tu, long and fanged and yellow-toothed, with the metal toe on his shoe, just the right one, meant for backs, shoulders, elbows, bone, sinew, body, the very reach and portal of the soul. He did not know if it were Poe or the quickened sound beyond, a noise in the night, like the swagger stick striking on another back, across the barest of another's flesh. He and Fortunato, he and the captain, the captain and Fortunato. Where did it end or begin? He could hear his old professor, John Norton, reading the passage, coughing his cigarettes into the paragraph, posing his hand between belt and self, sitting on the edge of his desk, nodding at the words, his voice alive, the Tower Bell ringing at the end of class, May smothering him with trees and the promise of evening coming at the break of day and all the day long, like a line at a theater queue, Humphrey Bogart on tap, Henry Fonda, Orson Welles, Jimmy Stewart, a host of floating faces and known voices carrying their own music, their own tempo.

His voice repeated itself: Caught between the professor and the captain!

It was at him again. The then and the now. Still, he clasped that finger and that thumb, those entities in the darkness, poised, relentless, waiting. Hunger, he realized, would accompany him all the days of his life. Oh, such weariness it could sustain. A being in itself. It would never change. No matter how many times Ping Tu kicked him, no matter how many times the stick flashed in the air and he could feel its slash before it hit his skin, the void in his body would reassert itself, the ever-calling vacuum, wanting, needing, crying for food, more food, decent food, one solitary piece of rye bread soft enough for his teeth where he held off the pain. It would do no good to get pain there, in his teeth.

If he let it in it would be with him forever. He'd suck it out of his teeth before he'd let it come at him, gnawing its way home, coming like an insidious disease, taking over, controlling, as conscious as breathing. Suck the teeth dry of pain, that was the trick. Call on perseverance repeatedly. Make it stand-to. A man-made demands on his body, on his complete self, the ego and the muscle, the sinew and the thought, the search and the grip. The echo came in the back of his head, even if it had to be that way until the last day. What he feared most was the lack of measurement, the inability of allowing or creating reference points, two points around time, time at the center of two points as distant as stars. There was that hunger for the sight of stars in this room without aperture. That hunger was there like an organ of skin, enveloping.

It was déjà vu, it was a turntable event. The sound came once more. He stiffened. Again. It was closer. Again. His whole body knew it was closer. It was not just in the hearing. It approached. Again. It made inroads. Again. It said so. The metal too. Again. The kick. Again. The slash. Again. Ping Tu smiling through his teeth. All over again. Oh, would Ping have a thirst for amontillado! Oh, were he himself the finest of stone masons, setting Ping Tu up for the full sentence; to make an end of my labor, to force the last stone into place; to set the best of mortar, forever.

"Yo!" he said into the darkness, quickly alert, his voice making an attempt at strength, soldierly, once again in the ranks. His mind leaped another leap. The finger and the thumb! No matter what joy comes, keep the finger and the thumb deployed. Be vigilant. Be ready. Anew came the full shiver. A shot of joy few minds would ever understand came over him. Alive and alert was he, down to his contriving toes. Oh, one grasp. One grasp! Oh, but for Christ, one grasp.

Then, as if timed by some legitimate god, a god of the deserts, a god of the deep unknown, a moan came out of the darkness, serious, cutting, soul-filled. It arched through his body. The rotted vest, the filthy piece of cotton beneath him, felt cold as stone, as hard, and as brittle if he moved an inch the wrong way, crumble and shatter its promise. Once more he was penetrated and violated in the darkness. Ache was in his soul, he was positive of that. It had a presence he thought immeasurable, untouchable. But here it was, at him, in him, with him, paining him as no pain had ever come to him.

Even yesterday, when Ping Tu had kicked him so many times that he lost count, where the metal plate in his shoe was now felt anew, was not as bad as hearing that moan, knowing Ping Tu at new carnage and employ, speaking indirectly to someone's mother. It nearly cost him his concentration. The finger flickered, tremulous, came back to place and the organ of his skin searched its wide expanse for the presence of vermin nearing that vise. Courage came anew, and vigilance, determination. There would ever be the thought of mortar setting in place, a cry lifting itself to the limits of the universe, a metal toe plate rusting back to its beginning.

He thought his eyes had closed for a moment, that sleep had come in the place of Ping Tu, that the moans and other sounds faded into the stiff darkness, lifted off to a distant place, yet to be remembered with vivid clarity.

Sleep had come. He woke, this prisoner, stood up roughly with ache anew, stiffly and absentmindedly slipped the rotted vest off his torso, and removed the remnant pants torn at the crotch, torn the length of one leg, letting the frayed string belt fall away. He dropped them and the worn cotton blanket into a tattered cardboard box at his feet, and, in an habitual manner, kicked the box under the cot.

In dawn's first precious light, he looked at his brother's picture, the major's leaf on his collar, the distance in his eyes, his brother six years a prisoner of war, dead of an abrupt stroke on the rescue plane, never to come home.

He touched the picture frame, cool in the first sparkle of light, spoke the words again, as he had every morning for more than a year, and stepped into the shower, the words echoing, beseeching, apologetic in the bedroom behind him: I know, Charlie! I know! I know!

Evan Stalworth's Wealth of Words

I'll have to tell the story because I'm the one most at fault here. I should have known better, I'm the new generation type. Even on the way home from the cemetery, going back to the house with my mother, my two younger brothers and my sister, it was me who should have known better. Lots of things should have tipped me off; instead of being bigger, having more room with a body gone from it, the house appeared smaller, at least to me. It felt smaller, smelled smaller, corners were tighter, the air cooler. I swore, after spending my first twenty-two years in it, it didn't have its hand out for me, "Not a touch in the tally," as my father used to say about things found useless, unproductive, too much emptiness to expend much-courted energy on.

My father's name was Evan Stalworth, a writer of sorts, and once had been a Marine, and stories about the Corps were usually reserved for male audiences. The writing bit began in late years. He'd retired early; what had obviously built up in him for most of his life had somehow gathered into form and was finding a way out of the sepulcher he had devised over those years to hold his material. I don't know how many times I had heard him say to my mother, in those explosive years after he'd found the computer, "Hey, Artis, you ought to read this piece I just finished."

He'd say it once, you could count on that, and then you could picture him waiting for the minute or so of silence. You'd hear the promise of exasperation from my mother, "There's plenty of time, Evan. I've things to do now. I'll get to it bye and bye." There was sewing to be done, cooking, work on her afghan for the Ladies Society. She didn't have a lazy bone in her body, nor was she mean. I think she heard little of what he said about writing ... as if it didn't really count, or amount to anything important, nothing like hanging with pride an afghan turned to the last twist of the wrist. An afghan was known and understood.

But then, in that small aftermath, a chair would creak, he'd swing it back in place in front of the computer, push a key, start again. That happened a lot of times those days. I can hear the weak echo of her words; I can hear the creak of his chair. All that day, all those days, he'd not say another word, at least not vocally. It was the routine for most of the recent years. And there were so many mornings, before me and Teddy and Gus, and Janny last, had moved out of the house, that Evan Stalworth, late bloomer, early riser, would be at the computer at three o'clock in the morning.

I'd come home for a quick visit from clear across the country. He'd beg me to make a CD of his material. It was, for me of course, a piece of cake. I did it in seconds. I did it every time I came home, which was at least three or four times a year. I never read what he had written. I was a technocrat, a new generation guy who loved the computer in my own way. It was not the memorial way of years that my father was carrying on with.

Teddy was a salesman and was damn good at his work. He came by every month or so, would stay for a few days in the old bedroom, do a few odd errands or maintenance chores, paint a hallway or wallpaper or hang some curtains, and move on. He was making lots of money and kept at it. Gus, driving his special bus for a big-time sports personality, rarely ever came home. Not even at Christmas. When he did drop by, there'd be a crowd of people gathering because they all recognized the big-time coach's bus, and Gus was able, in his own way, to get a few perks worked off for his folks. Janny had four kids of her own and tried, really tried, but it was tough to get home from Oregon where her husband Charlie, after years in the Navy, settled down. It was too expensive.

But, as it happened, none of us were readers. And we had all heard, growing up, some of the old gent's stories, "Evan Stalworth's Wealth of Words," as we and some neighbors had come to call it, the pleasant parts of some late evenings on the porch or in the kitchen hunched over a few pops of coke or beer. It was old hat to us. And it was a shame that we had not listened more closely. But isn't that what we learn in life, and usually when it's too damn late?

So, the day came, and the day was announced with a thunderstorm and me in a plane and the captain sounding nervous. I promised I'd get home before the day was gone to say hello. The promise stuck. I came around the corner late at night in a rental car and saw the flashing lights of an ambulance and the companion fire truck. It was Evan's heart. He didn't make a big race out of it. Just took himself into a final silence, and was gone.

All of us were there the next day, Janny coming last and Gus picking her up at the airport.

My mother made only one demand when we came back from the cemetery. "Now, while I have the help, get all of his clothes out of here and gone to Goodwill or the homeless. I don't care where as long as someone can use them." She added, a small token of explanation, "It's what he'd want."

We did all that in short order, in green bags and dumped them in a collection point. Useless, worn clothes and all kinds of underwear and socks by the dozens we threw out in the trash. Mom pushed us. "I don't have the hands I used to have. Nor the legs. It has to go now. Give those old coats and those jackets to the homeless. Every last one of them. Those old hats of his, baseball caps by the dozens. His winter boots and fishing boots and his fishing poles. Give them to Harry next door. Give Harry his tools if you don't want them. I'll never use them." She was practical, and realistic, down to the last handkerchief in one of his drawers, the last pair of pliers on a shelf.

That full day we moved as a team. The house, I'm afraid to say, started to grow again. Rooms leaped in size. Corners gleamed like they hadn't in years. The cellar and garage grew themselves three times over. Space tripled up in an hour's time. It was a kind of new-birth glory. It happened all the more every time a corner came back from where it had been hidden for years, and a one-time crawl space came exposed and a section of the garage she had never been in showed itself off.

Then, after all that acute labor had been expended on the house, to free up what one might call the debris of a lifetime, there remained only the small room he called the study. It was where his third generation computer rode the edge of his desk, the one I had bought him and shipped home from one of my trips. His first computer was stuffed under a supply desk in a corner, its innards frozen for all time. The second one, one that I had worked on a few times and glimpsed but a few lines of his work, also went astray the day he got the latest one I sent, the one with the narrow console he thought was the next wonder of the ages. He had leaped at that one. I had made him CDs for of all his stuff. He told me he wanted a title printed on it. "Evan Stalworth's Wealth of Words Most Memorable." I had softly smiled to myself, loving his ideas, but not listening really… I was a CD maker, cut and dried! A tool merely. I knew my place in all of it.

In one corner of the room, in a closet, on packed shelves, stacks of papers had gathered and grown over the years. He must have spent all pre-computer days doodling on those papers.

Mom said, "What about all this stuff?" She looked at me for the answer.

I said, "He said it was all on the CDs I made. He had me transfer everything. There'd been a whole bunch of files. A whole bunch. I don't know how long it took him to do it all, but it's all on the CDs." I smiled, "We had about a dozen CDs. I made one of his whole system every time I came home. So much repetition, duplication, but he didn't want to miss a word."

The judgment was quick. "Get some bags, boxes, anything," she said. "Move it all. We can decode, decipher, read the CDs some other time."

We swung into action. The room leaped into life. Walls loomed in clear patches where piles of paper had hidden them for years. Teddy promised to paint and wallpaper his next trip. We moved a history of a man into bags and boxes and into barrels. We rushed. Mom kept looking at her watch. "It's trash day. It can all go now if we hurry." It was near three o'clock in the afternoon, destiny calling.

It was done. Outside the gears of the trash truck groaned in concert with weights. The grinding mill of its hydraulic gears swung the overhead crusher into the life-spill of papers. A piece of 8 ½ x 11 paper flew on the quick breeze and landed in Harry's yard. He had been watching his friend being moved out. He picked up the piece of paper, looked at it, shrugged his shoulders and put it into his empty barrel. Toward the back of his house he walked, toting the barrel in one hand.

While the others were outside, watching the truck move away, I plugged the first CD in. There was one message. I have nothing memorable. The CD was empty. The same message came up on each of the twelve CDs. I have nothing memorable. I was shocked. Turning, I looked at the other computers. The emptiness fell down through me. The weight of years and piles of paper and powerful gears and awesome forces pushed down through my whole body. Oh, this awful retribution, this reprisal.

I knew. Oh, I knew. If I mentioned it to my mother she'd raise a hand and say, "Today's not the day. Time for that later, in the bye and bye."

I heard the echoes. I heard the chair squeak, the key being punched. I didn't say a word. There'd be time for that later on.

It was four or five months later. I was heading out of Waylom Village deep in the tip of Michigan. I was passing a gasoline or oil truck with a flat tire. A small service truck was parked behind the big truck. Sun glinted on the bumpers. Two men were talking. The sun was also descending a hillside, tossing shadows aside. I could smell, not oil or gasoline, but honeysuckle or new cut grass or the edge of a barn's existence, a birthing of one kind or another. Perhaps it was promise itself. A flock of birds was a small cloud against the sun, but only for a second. The radio was on and the man I occasionally listen to when I am in this part of the country was talking:

I swear I never heard his name before, but I know all of you will hear of it someday. I found these pieces in a new, small magazine. Some of the finest, grandest writing I have ever seen. We have to get this man here. We have to listen to what he says. It is most remarkable. It is brilliance itself. These three pieces are all I have. I hope I can get more. I hope I can get all of it, these things he called My Memorable Stuff by Evan Stalworth. Does anybody out there know him? Call me at this number....

"This is what I'm going to do, and I'll tell you right up front so he can hear me too, him who's back there in the trunk of the vehicle where I got him all tied up and a mask on him so he ain't seen a glance of me, I can tell you that much. Here's the lay of the land; I'm gonna take a bullet out of my pistol, this here mad-ass .45, heavy as a rock it is, scratch his name on the shell casing if I can spell it right, then I'll reload, then I'll aim it right between his eyes so that your precious Signal Corps civilian horse can see what's coming, the bullet that's gonna kill him. How's that grab you? More than the friggin' movies themselves, huh?. Plot thickens, huh? More than a lot of those dinky writers have made that statement; it's all over the place, but I'm gonna do it! That's a damned promise, my lady friend! I'm flat-out gonna do it, you screw this up on me."

He paused, the Signal Corps operator at one end, Julianne Dawdry, recognized the pause, and so did Jeffery Kincaid, III, a civilian attached to the Signal Corps of the U.S. Army in Germany, trussed up in the trunk of the car, his hands bound at his chest, his head covered with a partial mask that kept his eyes closed but allowed his ears to hear this end of the conversation.

And that one-sided conversation continued: "I have left 30 written directions in 30 places of public trash collection barrels all over the city of Berlin. Them Heinies call them *Grüne/Blaue Tonne* (green or blue cans) for paper and cardboard recycling. The instructions say that in one of these places, along with an old pizza box to swing the Italians into it and to make it like a sign for me, you're going to leave one million bucks, in no size bigger than $100 dollar bills, in one of the 30 places or a new one I select within 5 minutes of my next call, which, of course, I won't say when it'll come to you, before you share that with the German gendarmes too, but none of you know what kind of a truck or car I'll use for delivery and/or pick-up, like UPS German style, or Blitz Delivery as BD is called hereabouts like it's a brand new idea but it sure as Hell ain't if you look back only about three quarters of a century, my math bein' kind a touchy."

Jeffery Kincaid III heard every word of this end of the conversation, heard the engine start up, the gears shift momentum, felt the vehicle grab a chunk of paved road, and take off again, as it had so many times in the past hours, getting tired of it all even at rest. He'd been able to tell a few places in the city by smell or sound but none being sure identifications and certainly not specific enough to provide rescue instructions.

He listened to the engine, heard a familiar hum, thought it to be a U.S. made Ford of fairly recent vintage. He added that to his collectibles: perhaps a Ford, certainly a .45 in the mix, a false German voice that handled English like a poor school teacher, and some areas of Berlin itself that came from no more than a few smells or sounds.

His own list was growing. He had almost said "file" or "folder," laughed at himself, knowing it was a carry-over from his computer training. The laugh, hushed within the mask, made him feel better. Nothing's better than a laugh. He'd need more of them, to be damned sure. He tried, with difficulty, to ready himself for added humor from whatever source.

When he suddenly realized the vehicle had entered a gas station, the odor devil strong, Kincaid perked up in the car's trunk, but finding no way to bang on an inner metallic surface of the vehicle.

Instead, he paid strict attention to any outside conversation, with a new voice saying, "Yuh, I was mustered out while stationed here and married a girl from the Mitte section just down the road. Yup, 22 years in the service before I cut the strings. Even got a grandson now, living with us, 8-year old car lover. Every night I get home, Donny, that's his name, named for my brother lost in the war, asks me what different kinds of cars I serviced during the day or ones I worked on. I'm a mechanic too, not just a pumper of gas. He keeps a list of car names and stuff about them, loves SAABS, Fiats, Mercedes-Benzes, Audis, BMWs, Renaults, Volkswagens, you name it and he knows it. That means he knows engine data, model and year numbers, you name the vehicle and he can spit out a whole paragraph of stuff and he's only 8 years old. Can you imagine that. He'd know this rig of yours is a U.S.-made Ford Edge, 2007 model. Donny'd even ask the plate number case he ever saw it he'd know I worked on it. I can see your first 4 plate numbers, 6179, but not the last two because you've been banged in the back end. You catch the dog that did it?"

Great laughter outside. "Hell, how did you know that? It was an old lady with a little dog who pissed in her lap at the same time, maybe caused the accident. I laughed like hell and let her go. Didn't want to get caught up in any mess. And that's quite a feat for an 8-year old kid who might run this place someday."

"Wouldn't be his worst choice, his father off in the army, his mom in a drug rehab place, life tough enough as it is."

Kincaid's list had jumped with a ton of information.

Down the road the driver made another call and the unheard response of the Signal Corps corporal at the switchboard had summoned her captain. "It's him again, captain, still with Jeffery bound and battered I'd bet. Says he knows we called the police, which he expected, but he's still incommunicado on the streets of the city with a half million other vehicles, won't ever say car or truck, I'll bet. Says he's getting ready to pick his spot and has seen enough strangers around to know he'd be spotted so he's prepared to change delivery and pick-up destination in a flash."

Kincaid, still inert, still bound and masked in the trunk of a U.S.-made Ford, would have been able to concur with her deductions. He wondered about the million dollars in a package with no bill bigger than $100, and an old pizza box ... why not a favored German quick-meal, like *Eisbein* (Pork Knuckle) at Zur Letzten Instanz in Mitte. He figured the driver had an Italian background, a family connection, a favorite vacation spot he might certainly visit again, if things went right for him, and went left for himself. Kincaid managed a hushed laugh, and began to review his list of hints and facts obtained to date.

He was not empty-handed even though he was bound at the wrists.

Corporal Julianne Dawdry, on the phone since the inception, who had worked with Kincaid a number of times, who was adept at her work and the various duties of the Signal Corps, told her captain that she could determine some parts of the city by loud area sounds detected during phone calls, "but don't bet on me. I guess sometimes."

She continued, "I am very familiar with the basic parts or divisions of the city, burroughs or districts which are called *Bezirkes*. They are Charlottesburg-Wilmersdorf, Friedrichshan-Kreuberg, Lichtenberg, Marzahn-Hellersdorf, Mitte, Neukolln, Pankow, Reinickdorf, Spandau, Steglitz-Zehlendorh, Templhof-Schoneburg, and Treptow-Kopenick. I've been in all of them in my 10 years here in Berlin, where my mother was born.

"We've been in touch with the *Berliner Polizei, Der Polizeipräsident*. the German *Landespolizei* force for the city-state of Berlin. They are very cooperative and are ready for action or directives, as soon as we have a solution on hand."

Her pause was significant. "I must say that Kincaid is as good a friend as I have over here, has been that way for a few years, and nothing romantic about it, in case you're interested."

The captain, of course, knew better, was totally interested, and preferred nuptials over full disappearance of Kincaid and the mysterious driver of the kidnap vehicle.

It was a tight spot for all of them.

That friend Kincaid, at the precise moment, had discovered a small iron ring in the trunk of the car, a possibly loosened element from some lock connection; he wouldn't let go of it, thinking of some way to utilize it.

There was nothing else.

The gas station pumper was still talking as Corporal Julianne Dawdry raised her hand and directed her boss to listen; both of them heard the tiny, tinkling sounds of metal touching lightly on metal.

"That's code," each acclaimed with astonishment, and heard, again and again, the same, faint message, tinny, tinkly, but ratta-tap tapping away: "blu us 2007 ford edge plate 6179--."

When the blue 2007 Ford Edge pulled up to a roadside trash barrel in Mitte, pursuant to directions from the kidnapper, and with the reception quickly planned, Corporal Julianne Dawdry couldn't hold back a kiss on the lips of Jeffery Kincaid III. Nor could he let go of her, even though the rope burns on his wrists still sent messages of their own.

I Am What I Am Not

Sometimes, a puzzle just has to be disentangled.

The voice, deep at times, sometimes a tone lighter, and usually female in its tenor, came out of the near darkness every night to Hobart "Hobie" Spurt, octogenarian, reader of clouds, fog banks, permanent tree disappearance, erosion, mysteries abounding in all of life. All the voice said was, "I am what I am not."

Hobie would sit on his porch or at his window looking down on the high tide of the river where it came to the foot of the First Iron Works in America, and in reflections cast off from the mirror surface see the dark images of the ancient Scottish indentured laborers at their work. They could run wheelbarrows of bog matter and iron ore with the best of the brickie laborers he had worked with in his youth. Sometimes he saw the flighty spirits and shadows of young boys, long-lost friends, who drowned while riding the winter-time buckeys or ice floes on the Saugus River. Once he saw a man trying to push with difficulty a piano down an embankment into the river. He thought nothing of it and weeks later heard that the man had been missing for weeks. He never thought of it until the night the voice came again.

The sadness grazed him, at times invaded him. But when each of them was accompanied by the mysterious voice, the voice out of darkness, the figures seemed to come alive for him.

And the words were always the same; "I am what I am not." Never different, "I am what I am not." No change in the enunciation, he believed.

"I am what I am not."

In the morning, at the side of the porch where the voice seemed to issue from, he found an old twisted piece of rope perhaps the neighbor's dog had brought in, the dog always gnawing at something, like a pup working its teeth into shape. The dog had been busy, it appeared, because it was not the first time that such a gnarled piece of hemp was found on his property and was obviously from some mooring down at the river, a line rotted or broken loose by strain or chewed away from its task.

The night he saw one of the lost boys whip off his jacket and holding one sleeve of it, tried to toss the other end to his friend who had slipped off the buckey into the water, he saw their faces as clearly as if they were on the other side of the window, looking in at him. And the voice was there, with them, beyond the glass, somewhat muted, but enunciated clearly: "I am what I am not." Both of the boys were lost and the voice fell silent for the time being; enough pain for one night, it might have said, though Hobie could not believe that possibility.

Again that night he prayed for them, hoping it was the illusion of a haunting from the witching hour at the end of a bad day, the distaff side of a nightmare. And nothing more.

But the voice from darkness said with repeated fervor, "I am what I am not." Different words were stressed at different hearings, with his attempts to pin down what was really being stressed.

Yet he also realized that he'd never been hurt in all of these scenes, these offerings "from the other side" had never been threatened by this … this … Whatever.

There were evenings that Hobie dared not go to bed, fearing he would miss an episode where a lost person was found, came back, was whole again. One of those evenings he saw one of the Scottish serfs slam another laborer over the head with a shovel. It was not boys playing around on the edge of darkness.

It was real stuff, but perhaps only real in the mind.

And where else, mind you, can it be? he wondered, the tone in his voice, the intent, the outcome, giving him a small touch of humor. But it was hardly worth a laugh, though he did manage a small one.

And with that scene came a scene with Hobie in it, drawing the mysteries into such a relationship that seemed to drag him into a significant enlightenment. He was 20 at this sudden reoccurrence, digging in a trench of the reconstruction of the Iron Works on its way to becoming a National Historic site, when his shovel unearthed a human skull, the skull with a break in it where one ear had been. Yet, in spite of the true sight down in the trench, he swore someone spoke. "At last," a voice said, as if they had been waiting for Hobie. Though he tried, Hobie could not fend off those words.

The archeologist of the site said, in an offhand way, "Sure looks old. Sure looks like an accident happened to the old buck and he somehow got buried where he fell. See that dirt about him, that's clear sand, that's almost untouched, virgin soil. He must have been digging here and died here and the wall of the trench must have fallen in on him."

More pith than pity in those words, Hobie thought.

Oh, a soul cast adrift without a simple prayer.

For over 60 years the discovery of the skull and other bones had bothered Hobie --- until the night, right from his porch, he saw that skull get hit with the blade of a shovel. Of course, it was 60 years too late to say anything.

The night of his 84th birthday, warm for late winter, the voice called him again, the call the same as ever, the words the same as ever, only the mere tone of them with an edge of difference; "I am what I am not."

It was well past midnight for him and for his due sleep when the words came. He felt bad, as had happened before in recent incidents, and put on his slippers and went outside. The high tide in the river was catching lights from the police and fire station, red lights from traffic control bouncing off the river's smooth surface. Eternity itself sat in the widening sky without measurement except for the river disappearing behind the slim shadow of Round Hill and the sky disappearing behind Vinegar Hill, Indian remnants in one place, pirate gold and jewels in the other, each with revelations yet to come.

"I am what I am not," said the shadows, said the voice, now husky. A forgotten movie actress made a face for the voice, dark hair hanging in a lovely mass, one eyebrow arched, her lips pursed for kiss or curse, he was not sure. Then he stepped once more on a twisted piece of rope.

"Dog's at it again," he said. "Klem's been down to the river, at the moorings." The vision of the black and white spaniel came up behind his eyes. "I've got to get down there someday and see how many boats have floated off because that damned dog's been chewing on their lines." He smiled as he imagined a few dories, lobstermen's dories, loose on the river, the tide going out, and the dories on errant rides, the hardy lobstermen waving and yelling frantically on the pier as if each loose dory had a passenger aboard.

Hobie kicked the rope off the patio and onto the driveway pavement.

"I am what I am not," said the voice again, as if he had kicked someone in the rear end.

Then, as if to change his train of thought, night overpowered him with its beauty, stars like shooting galleries had unloaded all their ammunition up into it, or like golf balls sparkling on the local driving range and the recovery vehicle was out of order. He laughed again at his images, thought about the numbers of ropes that had appeared beside his house, thought about the voice coming at him so clearly that it was more than a message.

It was, he thought, a statement from a deity, a godhead, some being from beyond his understanding, beyond his experience, beyond any bounds of logic, but saying something that counted. A command? A plea? A bare statement?

"Perhaps," he said, the humor still finding its way in him, "it's a witch." He added a stern pronouncement as he carried himself slowly up the stairs to his bedroom, "Aha, I am caught up in witchery. I wonder if it's a good witch or a bad witch, like the good witches of Oz, Glinda and Gayellete of North and South or the bad witches, Nessarose and Elphaba of East and West".

There was a difference, known or unknown, in all of them. And that made him say, aloud as he plied his way one step at a time, "It might have been in her tone, or the way she stressed one word ahead of another one time and then stressed another word in a later message, but each message coming with the same words."

Slippers off, about to go to bed, some sudden clarity of his questions came rising as if it had followed him up the stairs to his room.

It made him yell.

"There is a difference!" he exclaimed. "There is a difference. I've found it! I've found it!" His mind had leaped up from a soggy mass to find the bright light and he went back down the stairs.

In the driveway he picked up the clutter of rope he had kicked aside. He grabbed it in one hand, unrolled the twist in it and the voice said, so that he understood it perfectly, "I am what I am, Knot."

A shift came, a surge in his hand, and a most beautiful maiden formed before him, the maiden he had dreamed of all his life, and she kissed the old man on the lips and said, "Knot thanks you for her freedom, for untying her, and will remember you all her time."

And she was gone into another world.

The Last Tree Standing

For starters, it was devastation, wide as the continent, harried, hurried, invasion from the depths of all significant bodies of water, those landlocked and those not, come shoreward a titanic force and right behind it the New People with unheard of powers, suppression their game, all-out suppression. The land rocked with changes,

Old prospector and traveler Alec Perfed, separatist for almost half a century, wide-eyed like his known two blue oceans, broad shouldered and thick-chested, still a dreamer of the old days before the New People arrived in mysterious clouds of fog and mist and wide-water upheavals from wherever in the semi-darkness of one insidious evening, had been absolutely delighted and surprised to discover a tree in a crevice in the Teton Mountain Range.

He hadn't seen a tree in two years and knew the timing to be correct.

Measuring time on a piece of an old pool cue stick stuck in a leather sheath on his mule, he was more than a month of marks into the third year when he first smelled the tree and then spotted it in the slight crevice where it had started and leaped slim and desperately high seeking the rays of the glorious sun, vitality moving two ways at once, at once powerful and pleading. He admired the birth and growth of the tree against all the odds. Promise, pride, the sudden burst of passion in him said it would be, forever, a story to be told,

For three days of celebration he sat against its trunk, sipping water from his canteen, sharing drips and drops of it with the base of the tree, loving again the connection, his mind loaded with thoughts now and then coming fuzzy, now and then choir clear, as the rhythm of the tree's life surged through his tissue and muscle, graced his bones, said that love still lived inside, that the Old People still had a chance at revival, survival.

Above all, the tree was a Godsend, a message so dear it almost exploded in him, the charge long and lengthy and full blown in his frame. On a sudden spurt of energy and mind, he observed from several viewpoints, each one quite decisive, how special this tree was, an oak appearing like no oak ever revealed. From hidden images that deployed in various parts of his mind, he saw every other oak as hunchbacked as Quasimodo, broken-armed, distorted, a simple convolution of growth, limbs everywhere awry, twisted, cross-bowed and cross-linked, crooked as a thief bent on awful errands and commissions, proud, stubborn, muscular against nearby pines and maples, making way in the face of all the deciduous and coniferous allies of the forest, king of many lawns and lays of land, trunk solid as the nose-guard of a Super Bowl winner, residing under the hide of a rhinoceros or crocodile, armor-borne, impenetrable, immoveable, yet at periodic instances might provide yield.

Yet this lone tree was different by every degree: dream-like, sylphic, the silken, long limbs stretching far overhead, hunger's reach for passion of performance, a ballet dancer caught on stage by a photograph in a second of maneuver, a brief copy of her elasticity and grace, her limbs on one tiptoe and stage-oriented for this single and lone observer, and inarguably fateful from the outset of observation.

For a moment he felt as special as the lone tree stretched out for its life, its very cause ... of which, it also said, Perfed had lone control over its existence.

Out of that mind set, in a quandary, arguments in range, he shifted again, distractions beginning to work him endlessly. Coming in soft cushions of thought, in self arguments, were other wonders and awes; he missed his wife Melody and the country songs that had mated them in the first place, him coming from the northern edge of the Atlantic, her carrying the heart of Nashville, the guitar in her hands, nearly the best of late evening gifts. He had not seen her since the big wave came crushing and taking all he owned, but he remembered how she sang her songs, every one of them; loaded with suspense and promise for the late evening, the middle of the night, dawn pulsing with the same arrangements.

If he met a solitary soul in the mountain, his personal introduction would begin on a simple note and turn complicated when any conversation took place. Too often people held back, trust thin in such thin ranks. There were times, however, when Perfed was received elatedly and he'd reply, "I've traveled a long ways in my journeys, just as you have. I read that on you as though you sport labels."

He'd clear the air immediately, tie past connections to that other world they once had. "With me, I came from the murky waters of the Atlantic where my home was washed away on that first savage night on insular Nahant, now an island once more, Lynn off to the stern. Never a splinter of that warm abode seen again by me. The first great wave, water warmer than ever, at 90 plus degrees they tell me, had knocked a hole in the foundation of the house and took out of action every element with life, force or power by any and every connection, sending all to smithereens, and my Melody on an errand, beyond help, out on the causeway or at Lynn shore. Oh, we later heard stories that gained momentum about mountainous eruptions in the midst of all oceans and larger lakes, all at once as though a button had set them off, and surging landward with deadly force and steadiness, some waves, like tsunamis, standing up and rolling 40 and 50 feet high to the nearest coasts, nothing less than obliteration in their wakes. My home, on a ledge of rocks, its thousand pieces, went easy to that frenzy."

His head would shake with the recalled visions.

"I lit out of course, my wife gone, no one to hold me. In my early roaming, Maine-ward, New Hampshire, Vermont, New York, Pennsy, heading west, I skirted around places like Winnipesaukee, Moosehead, Sebago, Erie and the lower Great Lakes, waters presenting any significant size where far shores disappeared in vaguest mists, where new eruptions might occur. I subsisted on brook or stream fish at first, found or stolen goods cached in secret places by people who had already passed in the first year of The Extermination where The New People gathered in clusters waiting to break out and claim all the Earth.

"Oh, they were inventive, The New People, besides the way they had of killing trees, cutting lumber laser-like, a lightning-fast process, and that hideous supplanting power that took hold of whole cadavers of Old People and made new models in their new way, slaves for their bidding, like building new homes, working tirelessly, brought back from death to be drones or automatons. Frightening it was in every instance, like made-over mortuaries serving up plain servitude. At close looks I saw faces and the frames of old friends and relatives adapted into the new system, minus all the old connections. Each one of 'the recovered' had an alpha-number permanently scribed on their foreheads; such marked brothers, fathers, mothers, sisters and all along family lines are believably never welcomed by Old People no matter how deep their retreat is, most of them being in mountain ranges where the New People don't tread unless in army numbers, huge squadrons of them, much the way of the really old Flying Squadrons. That you've seen yourself, aye? It seems incredulous that they have their own fears. Think seriously on such a revelation. It could be a spoiler for us if we ever discover what it is, find the hook, the knockout punch, the great persuader."

On this particular day, the third day after he discovered the tree, he was ready for likable company, social hunger prodding him, beating at him. That's when a clanking but familiar sound told him he'd definitely have company ... a clatter of steel hooves on a rocky surface at a slow pace; "Time in no hurry to get any place on," as they might say. Not in weeks had he spotted anybody, and that last time across a wide canyon, the sun showing the man off as another wanderer of the land, nearly sequestered away, daring for a bit of sunshine, changing skin color with a new tint, feeling different about himself, at least trying to. But Perfed didn't hail the fellow. Unknown company up here had to be received with strict trepidation; perhaps that figure might be a scout for a "flying squadron."

With rapidity things happened closer to him on this occasion, air changing beforehand, a signal old as the past, ties coming along with it, seen, negotiated, connected. The sensations of past days possessed him with peculiar strength; at times he thought it to be loneliness. At other moments the old powers coming back to him by slim degrees. The old boisterous odors he loved and rosy scents in a new place, the quiet adventures, the soft romances of new days, the wet dribbles of love, hope eternal.

It all said this day was different too, as the sound grew louder. The first notes of a guitar chord slipped their way to him and he swore he knew the song but could not bring the name up. Then came a few words that captured the song title for him, one of Hank Williams' songs, a haunting from so far away and so far back it numbed him: "I'm a rollin' stone all alone and lost/For a life of sin I have paid the cost/When I pass by all the people say/Just another guy on the lost highway/Just a deck of cards and a jug of wine/And a woman' lies makes a life like mine/Oh the day we met, I went astray/I started rolling down that lost highway."

The mule appeared first as it rounded a bulging ledge on the face of the cliff, an oblong and dark head with aerial ears, and then Perfed saw the man suddenly waving a guitar overhead with one hand and with the other hand tap the mule on the head with a thin wooden prong, surely a long-held souvenir from the lumber wars. This was followed by a clear canyon-echo voice, his old acquaintance, Thorne Moraise, calling out, "Alec, I spotted you from a mile back. Any word yet? I'm anxious as hell for news and I'll settle for good or bad. Ain't talked to nary a soul in three months and been followin' your trail for a few days, your mule better'n my old Millie here. I sure hope you got a change of chew, a candy bar, an apple core. My tooth is pulsing like my heart. It ain't right. None of this is right, but we keep movin' on."

Another chorus of "Lost Highway" leaped off cold stone and warmed Perfed's heart, saving grace with timbre in it; moody and melodious and marvelous.

For openers, in cordial meetings, Moraise was boisterously hale, looked hard as nails, offered a solid smile when the gap closed between two men, and then, as though he might have forgotten, finally touched his hand over his heart in the truest Old People's acknowledgment. It was the old sign in a new place.

That simplest of gesture carried reams of belief in it, of promise, the salute, the announcement saying with its one tap, "All will one day be good again, good again for the Old People, the friendly ones, not the new ones, those alien critters from wherever the Hell they had come from, and bound to take over all of Earth."

The simple but encouraging tap on the chest, the way it was conveyed, was a gesture from those who intended to enjoy this Earth down to the last grain, the last blossom, the last fallen leaf, if such be the end, the hungry hanging on, the thirsty bent on digging new wells, the loneliest of them waiting in the new kind of mountains for the return of good Old Mother Earth to dance her old tune, swing to her own rhythms again, after the momentous swings of the Ages ... Stone, Bronze, Iron, Medieval, Industrial, however they hit her wide parts, her continents, islands, and outlandish elsewheres.

Perfed replied, tapping his own chest, past images floating magically and instantly between the two as though a movie provided the connection. Those two saw both oceans cupping them, green hills rushing up at snow-capped peaks, Florida jungles and Utah forests, the rocky Maine coast where endless blue stones stood in the way of the capricious seas, the sand dunes of the outer Carolinas, Oklahoma oil rigs silent as God could make them, all the places that work, vacation, war and wandering had taken the pair and their fair brethren of all races, breeds, medal winners, leaders of some sort at one time, and the down and out, often quite like a close-to-losing fighter in the ring, on his knees, his head fuzzy, questioning a rally finding way, and wondering if it would be worth it?

"What's happenin'?" Moraise said. "I'm glad to know why you're out here. You never did say the other times we met, too much goin' on then. I always look to my own protection on trail meets but knew it was you."

"Aye, I did see some of 'the converted,'" replied Perfed. "It forced me never to address or hail anybody encountered in the mountains, and there were some like me, until I saw the face of that person, determined him New People with the old form, a cadaver come back by some awesome power we might never understand.

"What else is goin' on?" Moraise said.

Perfed motioned to him and said, "I want to show you something special, a piece of promised brightness, I swear," and took him to where the tree, a normally rugged oak with clutches of fingers at odd ends and loose, grown up tall and forcefully graceful in its niche of stone, its growth forced long and lean and glorious by its slim, prison-like location.

Surprise and glee grasping him, Moraise's face lit up like a lamp on an old telephone pole, the glow honest and his whole frame showing a sudden freshness as though a target had been reached, he and his mule coming to a sudden stop at sight of the tree. Quick judgment said its roots apparently had lunged down through a rocky path to find water, to keep it alive under awed, enforced circumstances, and allow it to grow straight for the clouds in its narrow confine, a stretching reach for God's grandeur.

Moraise, aware of a momentous discovery, exclaimed loudly, "What the hell are we going to do with it, Alec?" His hand rubbed the bark like it was his lost woman, teased it, waited for response, his eyes closing with lost dreaminess, a shiver grasping him with more old stuff, making him spit out to his friend, "It never goes away, Alec. That's one thing we own and that's for sure."

"We're going to chop it down and stack the splits." Alec said, "before 'they' get it. Then we'll fire up a good blaze. We've seen thousands and thousands of trees dropped by New People's laser application, whole forests in a day, and lumbered in mind-shaking speed. Hell, every one we've ever seen, or used to see. If we look down from here we don't see a single one. This is it, Thorne. This is it. All of them cut before any of us could take a deep breath. We're going to celebrate it, this fantastic new discovery, this lone tree, piece by piece. We're starting a celebration of an odd sort."

With that declaration, in agreement, their axes were swinging, biting, chewing at the tree, the old rhythms quickly found by the pair. Back they went to the days of rising oil prices, purchasing wood-burning stoves, venturing into forests and hillside growths, into neighbors' yards for falling apple trees, cutting, splitting logs, stacking them in the yard, in the wood box, fighting against the increase of prices, loving the woods and forests and the comradeship of two or more ax men, at least two vehicles, two gas saws, such as Jonsereds and Husqvarnas, never alone in the woods, fishing on the way home, beer in cans, cheese sandwiches, now and then catching a trout in Pye Brook or under Thunder Bridge on the Ipswich River, temporary illusions of heaven, labor's payoff and contentment.

The good days.

It was Perfed's immediate decision right from the beginning of the discovery; this first tree seen in two years to be sacrificed for the old folks. From across the valley he hoped they'd come. Some of them to be Necessary Couples, those bound by oath to help the other as long as they lived, arrangements taking the place of marriage.

Perfed started a fire with a single match put to the shavings they'd sliced off one stick of wood. The welcomed warmth promised that it would last only a few weeks at most, but, as suspected, the thick, dark curl of smoke began drawing Old People off hidden places in peaks and high trails of the Tetons. They came, dozens of them the next day, to share the mystery, to warm their hands, to smell the smoke, to hear the old stories, a line of them emanating from peaks where new sleep spots had been located, hideaways for seekers, hunters, mountain prowlers, at times moving thin as shadows, those who could be mistaken for opponents counted on semi-invisibility.

The strange realization come to many of them in the gathering, as Perfed spoke, that individually and collectively the New People would not live in Old People's houses. "That habit, that trait, that unconditional issue, bothers me endlessly," he said, "for there's a reason built in it, a fright, an imperfection that might be harmful, frightful or infectious to New Folks. From this knowledge we might establish a weapon against them. Most all the trees across the land have been laser-cut as we've seen and lumbered for new homes in such a speedy manner it seemed unbelievable."

As he talked he fondled the bit of seed in his pocket.

Perfed went on to tell those gathered at this singular fire, "I made some experiments on my own, like tossing a handful of loam into a crevice or a cranny in the middle of a rock pile and grass'd grow while I was looking at the spot." And it all would end in his firm belief, "If we hang on long enough, we can beat them because there is something we had in our homes that frightens the New People to extreme measures."

Heads began to nod at that declaration; there had to be a way to confront them, beat them at their game.

When the fire would burn out, the last flame and ember dark as earth, the word on this tree had to go with those Old Folks when they finally departed from the final embers in guarded secrecy. The news, they trusted, might refortify at least some of the other Old People out there, but of course had to be kept from the New People.

Now, after the huge and momentous run-off of trees by the New People, old folks like Perfed could stand on a peak and not know the country out in front of them, not a tree in sight, the old Earth in a new curve out there, almost uncompromising, bald, bare, barren, a sight to frighten bold men. It was not the former land, comprised of places for animals, insects, the buzzing bee, the happy, lonely men like Perfed who could live and love necessarily the solitary life. But it was land without trees in succession like the pugnacious oak, dwarfed, weathered, and limbed to a kind of hell and back, or the gathered cottonwood centering their oases, or the pine and Douglas fir being the dress and gown and undergarments for a succession of hills and climbs for miles into and past the heat of horizons. Those horizons, every which way on Earth from most points, had always broadcast a calling for them as if they belonged over there instead of here, out there where squaw pine and deadwood lay waiting for fire watches, campfires, coffeepots at outlandish morning accents a man could live on during long nights of wait.

What they saw was different.

What came in place was a land of green lawns that ran for endless miles, the grass taking hold as if by a new magic and the oxygen produced from it was richer and cleaner than early oxygen. Grass grew, it appeared, in any clutch of earth no matter the size of the plot or the usual locations.

And far off, vaguely seen from the peaks, New People's tinned roofs reflected the specialized energies, the new communities glistening under the sun, fresh collections almost every day, spreading across the land, dooming what once was America to a particular and peculiar land of reflections, rays, glinting signs of an unknown energy from a strange source.

But no more trees.

None of them knew a seed had been cached in the pocket of Perfed's greatcoat. Of course, they'd want to make a ceremony of planting that seed and many of them would volunteer to stand watch as long as they could, until Kingdom Come, as some of them would obviously vow, still being cut the way they came into life in the old days.

Realizing the size of his audience, and to what extent he could sway them, agitate any of their complacencies, Perfed added to his speech: "There is going to be a war, perhaps a long war, but you must realize what I believe is going to happen.... Even though the New People are cutting all the trees to get lumber for thousands of new houses, they have no idea that once a tree comes down and the resultant lumber is used in construction, the first thing that arises will be the microbes and germs that the lumber brings with it right at the construction level. What they are afraid of is what they'll introduce to new buildings on their own; the first bit of dust tromped in, dropped food particles, shoe detritus from outside walks, will begin to infect their new houses. They are not immune to the extent that we are to the microbes and germs we've come to live with, as long as we followed decent habits of cleanliness. They really will fall to what they fear the most no matter how strong they appear, how smart and complicated, the obvious talents they have, yet are as simple as life."

One man jumped up and said, "That'll be forever. When does the war proper start? What should we do? I'm itching for action. All of us are tired of hiding out like forever." He balled one fist and pounded it into the other hand.

"Don't you see it yet?" Perfed said, rolling his eyes, looking outward over the grassy world, "They are infected as of now. I can feel it. It's bound to happen even quicker than we hoped, and even the final may take years but it'll be worth every day of it."

He raised one fist in salute and celebration, threw his head back, thrust both arms toward the blue sky and yelled out his newly favored slogan, "Robin will have Sherwood again," and the hearty, robust laughter echoed in the mountains all round. Some Old People danced, some sang, the fever caught up the ranks. The rocky background made it illustrious, notorious, the echoes running for mile on mile through the circuitous Tetons, as much "Hallelujah" as ever heard.

Before long the infections came, as Perfed vouched, and the New People, in a new hurry, began to fall flat on their faces as they rushed out of their homes, sick, bitten, ravaged to their worst fears. At first, when others came to help, they too fell ill and died quickly, with their adopted servants also immediately returning to their previous pasts. When such losses became unbearable for them, the New People caved in, panic ensued, and the new civilization was on its way off the face of Earth as swiftly as it had come.

When one seed sprung loose a tree from Mother Earth, right where Perfed had placed it, other trees began to grow nearby. The summer months enriched them as did the reach for water. With their growth assured, the forests started to return, their deep clutches welcomed by the riches of the land.

Eventually the stories came into the mountains about the final days of victory when all the seas and all the lakes and large bodies of water built up to new momentous eddies, whirlpools, vortexes and maelstroms, the water rushing in greater force than seen before. Such violent changes drew into their whirling hearts all the New People on the face of the Earth. They came, or were drawn by an enormous power, from every direction and from the longest distances, as if they too longed to be home again, in that distant place that sent them out in the first instance, explorers and settlers of another order, another place.

From high in his perch, Perfed looked down as New People's home became inhabited again, surely by the same unseen old microorganisms after a fashion, and by the Old People in heavy numbers enjoying new comforts for old bones. The wise men had always determined that there are many "good" bacteria in homes helping to keep the "bad" germs away. "Helpful microorganisms," they said, "overwhelmingly outnumber harmful ones. That's what the New People could not fend off. If you take away too many of the good bacteria it provides bad germs a chance to increase at a harmful level."

For a thousand years the Earth did not feel the wrath of invasion from another unknown source and Alec Perfed had long been encased in his favorite out of the way place in the Tetons. Once again he knew Melody's songs coming out of the Deep South, finding him for odd moments, awed times at old Nahant, but usually in the Tetons where he'd found his place of rest.

Black Bird of Prey, Death Ship II

The battle had been harsh, crude, and longer than expected, but at the inevitable end the ship Gerben Huraq had sailed on for three years, initially at the end of a sword honed to an invisible point in the hand of a maniacal privateer, was sinking fast. Huraq, still on the good side of thirty years of age and possibly primed for long distance of days, had once crawled up a rescue rope to that ship from another sinking ship.

Now, twice saved and twice accepted aboard a rescuing vessel, he was in the water again, and once more in the Black Sea, the sea of seas, death scene of floaters, those abandoned, thrown overboard or fallen from their stations at battle, each one in a downward slide into their own history. He had no idea how long he would last on this wide sea, until one precise moment when he espied through a break in sea clouds the growing dot of a mast at full sail advancing from a distant point, ever moving closer, hope most possibly at least a transient passenger.

A final surge of excitement propelled his nearly inert body towards an expectant welcome.

"Have I not lived most miraculously these long years," he said aloud, "the salt so new and fresh upon me, so far the sea barren for me except for the prospects of the oncoming ship, also a privateer no doubt, which has spotted me alone here on these waters."

Sooner than expected from his knowledge of the sea, the pure sound of a whistle, came to him across flat waters like a dog's master at summons.

Also caught in self-reflections came new admissions: "If I had advantages of a mirror, I would see on what manner my presentation makes to the master of this oncoming ship I now see sporting the Black Flag of our destinies, one more privateer abound at mission, commissioned by one's majesty, king or queen. We are the living dead as far as they are concerned."

"Ho, there, seadog," a voice called out, "if you swear allegiance to this boat and its captain, Slank by name, Jerdah Slank, once of Gorey in the Channel Islands, we will haul you aboard, feed you, and then put you to work for now until the holy Kingdom itself comes.

"We are a motley crew," continued the captain later, "and I am a master of its indifference. What say you and by what name are you called, either by friend or foe?"

With a dramatic move, illustrated by his uniform flaunting gay red and purple colors tinged with black edges on each piece, and sporting a wide-brimmed hat, Jerdah Slank fit the idea of a king of this small estate of a ship overrun and stolen twice in its career, and now sporting a name burned into its name plank, Black Bird of Prey, Death's Ship.

"My word is my agreement," said the swimmer, "for this water is not friendly at all. Please hurry me aboard. I fear only great tentacles from the deeps. I am called Gerben Huraq by those who know me and save me from certain death on this sea of deaths."

"... and my hand at the throats of those too hungry to abide my rules and destiny," being all he heard of the response from the deck of the rescue ship, a dazzling, bright, shiny brigantine, impeccable to its very corners and Huraq judging it to be as large as 150 tons, about 80 feet long with a crew of pirates as hungry as the captain. She appeared to carry a dozen cannons and would likely sport cargo space twice as big as the sloop he'd just come off.

This rescuing brigantine had two masts with square sails excellent for handling in a quartering wind and promising safe haven for an added good hand. The awed stories would soon come to him in secrets of the hold or in the rigging, away from other ears. A sense of clarity fed him its promises, though he felt a serious reserve manifest itself in the pit of his stomach; he forced himself to absorb that feeling in his guts.

Gerben Huraq, near exhaustion, too familiar with the destiny of lone swimmers on seas of the world, announced his obedience when he said, loudly, "I do."

As the ship came closer he realized it was a choice ship for battle rather than quicker and smaller ships, like sloops and schooners. He admired its way in the water, a sylph of a large ship loaded, no doubt, with more terror than The Deep itself. It loomed warm and welcome and he knew it could survive strong seas and storms.

He'd bet five toes it was built in a Dutch harbor.

In his mind he saw it commandeered, boarded, stripped of original crew and adapted as a new vessel under a new captain. To be sure, it was renamed on the spot, the old name erased, the new name scored into a mounted title board, a name to be known forever in annals of the sea. The ship was rugged enough to cross the Atlantic, and fair better than smaller crafts in harsh seas, now to be spoken in awe as Black Bird of Prey, Death's Ship.

When hauled aboard, he smelled the fumes of that scored naming, a new ship indelibly named, and of a recent encounter, blood evident on many edges, on innumerable surfaces.

He was roughly dried off, thus warmed and blood thickened, then ate and slept in deep leisure. When he came to he was in another battle, the guns firing away in two directions, fore and aft, sails rent, blood spilled, riches achingly at hand. They spent hours aboard the newly captured vessel, securing sworn transfers by the sword, caring for their own wounded, blessing those dropped to the deep, hanging the captain of that recovered vessel, scouring each and every space for stashed valuables, coveted trinkets, astounding gems whose quantity and unbelievable quantity tightened the crew in a hurry, and even a pet monkey promising larks and laughs on the coming voyages onto salty seas and Hells. The search was complete from stem to stern, prisoners freed and sworn to their savior, Captain Jerdah Slank, one-armed swordsman, gun carrier, fierce of beard, visage, voice, and a man who was not once alone aboard his own ship, sworn to be protected by two enormous black sailors, dubbed Shade and Shadow by the captain himself at their capture and life-long enlistment.

Huraq became friends with Shade and Shadow, at first from their lively laughter, twins at contagion and humor, and their looking for new friends, a new smile, a freshness come along with wind and water. Huraq fit the bill for them, a smile ready for one and all, even for the captain and his gentle black giant protectors who carried instant laughter at the back of their throats, timbered, husky, and waiting for employment. He found an internal gentleness in both giants who, at divergence of ways when scouring the ship for reason, stooped at every bulkhead, hands groping ahead of them around dark corners for unseen threats. Once, to their pleasant reactions when he tickled one such hand with an osprey's feather, their laughter filled the bowels of the boat, highly favoring this new man aboard.

And it was a time that shipmates began to disappear or get deposited at sea; some fell from the rigging, some pushed overboard, some poisoned and treated to a solemn sea burial, again over the side with a casual push.

It was also the time Huraq first heard from one of the twins about "the unfilled glove," which indeed filled him with curiosity, enough for him to ask directly of the giants. "If you note with care, you will find the answer you seek," one of them advised him. He pushed no more in that direction but began to observe all manner of actions and particulars on the topside.

One of those notifications he discovered was the stiff attitude of some fingers on the captain's left hand; the middle finger, the ring finger and the baby finger never moved, never touched any surface, grasped any object, signaled any intention. Huraq's curiosity was finally satisfied when Jerdah Slank sent him below to collect some charts from his cabin and he observed the collection of radiant gloves hanging on a line, the subject fingers of each left hand obviously stuffed with stiff contents, filling the shape of that digital home.

Once that day when the captain was in close discussion with the first mate, and the giant twins were at ease, Huraq said, "Shade and Shadow, I know about the missing digits on the captain's left hand. Can you enlighten me as to the cause of that condition? I am more curious than a mouse." He fully shrugged his shoulders as though he was lost at sea again.

Shadow, the most talkative of the two, and most daring, said in a soft undertone, "The words come from our mother who was at Gorey in the Channel Islands, both midwife and assistant to the lone doctor, one named Emil Parsentico, and his lover when his wife was killed by a runaway horse. For centuries we have had Voudun, or what you may call Voodoo, in our tribe in Ghana in west Africa, believing in one god and pleasing that god the best way possible enables good health and wealth to those fortunate enough to have Voudun expressed in their names, called upon them. We have met others like our mother across the seas in many countries or possessions of such countries. The bite in the snake of the belly or a bull with sharpened horn protects one from foes through all the days of belief in the spirits that surely possess them from the moment of birth."

Suddenly caught up in his brother's spirited views, Shade interceded and said, "Mother hurried off one day to assist at a birth when the doctor was treating a sailor who had been hauled from the sea. She knew the lady of means was in a bad way while the doctor was later delayed by delivering a baby with three fingers missing on his left hand. The doctor knew intuitively the fate that would fall upon the boy in his family, the father being a belligerent and bothersome man, so he took the deformed child with him in the night and swapped him in place of the lady of substance at the palace, calling upon our mother to sail the spirits with boy babies for their lives. The ill-formed child enjoyed the comforts of the castle and the other boy had the love of an unknowing sensitive mother and a father enjoying perfection of his child."

He paused and said, "Life, with one stroke, took divergent turns, and you know half the story, at this end."

"So," said Huraq, "the crippled child, with a spoiled life, became a pirate, our pirate, and the other ...?"

"The other became a favored son of somewhat gentle parents, the good product of the covering doctor who treated him all his early life, and our mother who was able to watch over him with the good spirits always at hand."

"Yet, our captain has his fifth boat, as I count from stories, and looks to become a most notorious privateer on the oceans of the world. Could it not have been otherwise?'

"Aha," proffered Shadow, "and you or me or my brother might not be here now, and our mother might be in another's servitude, a prison's worth of undue penalties for a gracious lady who looks under green or yellow stones, behind wind-pushed sails, and on the far side of the horizon, all for the best becoming our personal gains."

The smile that broke upon his face said he believed each word of his delivery, to such an extent that he made a sign of the cross over his heart, bowed his head and grasped a hand from each listener, passing on his current passion, faith, and future.

Captain Jerdah Slank, attentive to all activity, had espied the three in tight conversation, and commenced a diatribe none of the three had heard before, nor any of the pirates from deck through rigging, so loud did he exclaim; "I'll have no undue or malevolent partnerships, other than brothers of the blood, here on my ship," by which he had excluded the giant blacks for his own protection rather than theirs. "That is the law of the bridge, this bridge and this captain, and the law of the sea, and the law of my interdiction. Since that ungrateful slug pulled from the sea, the one named Gerben Huraq, I have personally counted 29 shipmates who have been dispatched from the ranks, all unto the gods of the seas, for one indiscretion or another from blatant treason to petty thievery of shipmates' goods and spoils, and none directly by my hand but by commission on him called Huraq, who looms next on the list, lest any man speak otherwise in defense of his maligned office, hereafter called "the night master of fate, the dark progenitor of the canvas-wrapped, silence-ensured poor souls cast to the deeps."

He let the pearls of his words fall to the deck on which he, as complete master of the vessel, let them shine in their abruptness and clarity as law of a captain of the main. And there followed not the silence of abeyance, the trust of the masses, the ghosts of lost comrades and shipmates, not the indecisive silence of the uprooted, the peculiar silence of the compromised and abject, but the voices of opposition.

Shade, first to speak, his hand on the shoulder of Huraq, a distinctively protective mode seen and understood by all the command, interpreted from the first word, said so softly that those in the rigging might have fallen to the deck in their leaning to hear defiance rise slowly but surely in the air, like a keen dagger held upwards in a formidable fist, "We are done with secret deaths of many of our comrades committed in a patch of darkness, as on starless nights, or often when the moon refuses to accompany us though we are secretly outward bound, but bound for riches. That singular man who cannot grasp a sword in his left hand falls far short of being a complete master of such a vessel and must take his place in the mode of all slavery," and with such quick utterance, the captain of a boarded ship, Jerdah Slank, was cast into ignominy aboard his 'own' craft, the devil himself be damned, too.

It was not too long before Gerben Huraq was master of his own ship, and he let the name stand in its place.

The Boy with a Crooked Mouth

It was never what he said, The Boy with a Crooked Mouth, but how he said it, the way he sneered and looked down at people, at people who did menial tasks. He looked down at maids, truck drivers, sheep ranchers and even firemen when there was no fire. He had little use for landscapers and log splitters, men who froze ice cream, men who climbed poles to put up wires or women who spent long hours making clothes for other people.

Whatever he said, the mean way he said it, the way the words came out of his mouth, made his mouth crooked. The words came with something almost visible hanging on them, pulling at his mouth, like spidery webs or tree moss or ghostly strings of a sort. And his mouth always got twisted and screwed up and made him look odd. He never once realized it. Nobody ever told him, "Go look in a mirror at the way your mouth looks whenever you talk." Nobody ever said to him, "Go talk to the mirror and tell us what you see."

They let him go on talking because his father was the richest man in the town. This was the town where the rich man lived on the top of the hill in the biggest house. It was the house, as The Boy with a Crooked Mouth would say, closest to the stars. "Some nights, if you don't know, I can almost reach out and touch my stars."

Words like those words really stretched his mouth out of shape and made him look so silly and so plastic that people did not laugh, they pitied him so much. "My stars!" they would say to themselves. "My stars!" sounding like, "My word!" and small glee filled their eyes. The Boy with a Crooked Mouth particularly liked Orion, sitting up there on top of everybody in the whole universe. Orion, he thought, must be much like his own father, princely, top of the mark, one of a kind. And, he often said to himself, the kind of a man I will become some day.

One day a new boy came into town. He was tall and had red hair. His bright eyes and handsome face put him in the limelight right away. While he walked about the town that was new to him, he whistled. Every place he went he whistled and people knew he was coming, or knew he was going. All kinds of whistle sounds came from his lips; long whistles and short snappy whistles and train whistles and bird whistles and bird songs, and even ship whistles sounding as if they were far at sea. When he did a whole song while whistling people would marvel at his range of notes and how beautiful the tones were.

When The Boy with a Crooked Mouth tired of all the attention being paid to The Boy Who Whistled All the Time, he walked up to him and said, "I bet you think you're pretty special the way you can whistle. I don't think you can whistle that good." He turned and pointed off to the house on the top of the hill. "I live up there. Where do you live? What does your father do for work? Does he work in the fields? Is your mother a maid? If she needs a job I might be able to get her one."

His mouth was as crooked as it ever had been. It was like a scar that had healed from a bad wound, or a bolt of lightning caught in its place in a dark sky. Jagged it was, and wretched. It made his eyes look funny and out of kilter.

The Boy Who Whistled All the Time did not answer the questions. Instead, looking right at the other boy, said, "Why is your mouth so crooked? Did you get hurt? Have you fallen on your head? Are you angry at me because you cannot whistle?" He stopped for a moment and looked closely at the boy's crooked mouth. "I doubt that you could ever whistle, your mouth is so crooked, so out of shape. It's as if it's bent or broken. I probably couldn't teach you how to whistle no matter how hard I tried."

"I can do anything you can do." Nobody had ever talked to him like this. It was strange. He wondered if he should look in a mirror, but he couldn't make himself do it. His mouth felt perfectly all right to him.

"Not with that crooked mouth," the new boy said. "You couldn't begin to whistle with a mouth like that in a hundred years." Off he walked, a glorious tune rising from his lips, a song that made people stop in their tracks, listen to the song, and remember the words that went with the music. A lot of them thought about olden times when they were young. All along the way people waved at him and raised their arms happily over their heads.

And The Boy with a Crooked Mouth saw it and wondered again about the mirror.

That night he talked about it with his father. "It'll come to you some day, my son," the father said. "You'll be able to whistle and you'll be happy for a while, but then, when it doesn't bring you any money or won't get groceries for you or pay bills, you might want to try something else." He smiled, patted his son on the head and said, "Like working in the bank when the right time comes."

"But what about this new boy? He keeps on whistling and he seems so happy and so are those who hear him. He doesn't have to pay any bills."

"Listen, my son," his father said, "Whatever you do in this life, just make sure people look up to you. Not down on you. That's what's important. Where you fit in this world."

"Like always living on top of the hill in the biggest house?" the boy said. Neither he nor his father saw how crooked his mouth had become once again.

One day the old gardener who worked on top of the hill at the biggest house carved a whistle out of an old piece of wood he had found. When he blew on it a beautiful sound came from it. He cut a few more holes and soon a host of lovely notes leaped into the air.

The Boy with a Crooked Mouth heard the notes and came running around the corner of the big house. The old gardener whose name was Renee Persimmon had always smiled at the little man of the big house. He had always been kind, and the boy knew it. Renee was one person he had no disrespect for, and did not look down on him.

"Where did you get such a beautiful whistle, Renee?" he said, and he sat beside the old man on a small bench.

"I made it from an old piece of wood. It was a pretty piece of wood, though. It had such a nice grain to it, long and smooth like a canoe or kayak or a swimmer in the water. I decided not to burn it and not to throw it away because most all things have some kind of use, are worthy in themselves."

"All things?" The Boy with a Crooked Mouth said. He listened to more beautiful notes coming from the whistle. "All things? Are you sure?" He did not know softness had begun at the corners of his lips. The music was still beautiful and Renee nodded his agreement. The boy said, "Will you teach me, Renee. I would love to be able to play that whistle the way you do."

"Why would you want that, Armand?" Renee said, deciding it was time to call the boy by his given name.

The Boy Who Once Had a Crooked Mouth said, "I think it would make people happy. It makes me happy. The Boy Who Whistles All the Time makes people happy." His lips were really soft now, and his mouth was no longer screwed up like a bolt of lightning or an ugly old scar. "Perhaps it would make my father smile to hear me play that whistle."

Renee Persimmon the old gardener said, "I don't think you need any lessons, Armand. You look like you can play it right off the bat. Here, try it," and he handed him the whistle and saw how soft and pleasant the boy's mouth was and how music would soon have its rightful place with him.

"Wait until The Boy Who Whistles All the Time hears this," he said as he played some beautiful notes. "It might be the beginning of a beautiful friendship."

"Yes," Renee Persimmon said, "an old friend of mine said that once in a movie a long time ago."

The Man Who Hid Music

One day at the little house where the dowser used to live a kind-looking man with a beard came carrying all he owned on an A-frame on his back. He set the A-frame on the ground and looked at the small house needing much work. Muscles moved under his shirt.

"Whose house is this?" he said to some children playing at an edge of a field. This was the place where the mountain came to a rest, but the river had not been found as yet.

One of the boys said, "It used to belong to the dowser, but he went away." The boy used a stick to walk with as one leg was slightly crooked and made him lean.

"Why did he go away?" the man said, looking closely at the stick the boy had to use.

"People laughed at him," answered the boy. When he looked at his friends some of them began to chuckle and grin. "Don't," the boy said. His sandy hair caught the wind; his eyes were hazel and steady.

"If I want to fix this house up and live here, tell me who I have to see." The children could see some of the tools hanging on the man's A-frame. On edges where the sun touched them the tools shone brightly as if they had been polished with gems.

"See Macklow the mayor. He lives down there where those walls meet." The boy pointed across the wide fields. "He'll be on his porch listening to the birds of the fields. My name is Max. What is your name?"

The man of the tools smiled at Max's description of the mayor. "My name does not count, only what I do," he said. He walked across the fields and soon had the house to work on. At first it was just the children who watched him fix doors and steps and windows, but soon other people, including Macklow, came to watch. All the time he used tools the man whistled different tunes. At his work he was a happy man.

The house was soon a sparkling and cozy place with no lopsided boards and no broken steps and no windows free to the air. When the man needed wood, he put the empty A-frame across his shoulders and walked off toward the mountain and the forests. In the evening he returned with a pile of wood of all lengths sitting across the back of his shoulders.

"Some day, perhaps soon," he said one day to the children watching him, and a few of the older people, "I will have a surprise for you." As usual, just at dusk, the man took some of his wood he had been working with and brought it inside the little house. The light went on inside so they knew he was still working.

Nobody knew what he was working on. But the light burned long into many nights.

And soon, to everyone's surprise, a garden was also blooming behind the house. Macklow was really surprised because his own fields were slow. Nobody had seen the kindly man walk out of his little house at night, time after time, and put buckets of water on his little garden. The dowser's well was right inside the little house and those who had laughed at the dowser never knew about the well and the sweet water it gave up.

One morning the man came out of his house and gave a new stick to Max. It was much better that Max's old stick, and was smooth and polished and very strong. Max was proud of his new stick and could walk faster with it. Over his head he waved it and showed it off to his friends.

On each morning from then on the man began to build a fence around the house and the garden. At first he put up strong posts, then mounted stringers between the posts.

When all the posts and stringers were mounted and connected, he began to place upright pickets on the stringers.

Now and then one of the pickets would cause someone to laugh and titter about its strange shape. Some of the pickets were not as pretty and straight as others. Some indeed looked odd and out of place. But the man kept adding both straight and odd-looking pickets to the fence.

"See," Macklow said one day when village people were talking about the fence, "he brings out what he brought into the house the night before. What he does to it is a mystery, but let us not laugh at him. We laughed at the dowser and he went away in the night. This man is a kind man and has promised us a surprise. Do not laugh at him, no matter what his fence looks like." When he looked at little Max with the new stick, Max and Macklow swapped nods, as if they shared a secret.

But laughter, though, did come each day, at the way the fence looked, at crooked or bent pickets, at the weird shapes of some of them.

Then the day came when all the vegetables in the garden were ripe and the bizarre fence circled the house. The man seemed pleased and put his tools down except for one knife and walked off toward the forest. He came back with one small piece of wood. From that piece of wood he whittled a small whistle. When he blew into the whistle he found only one note, a pure note, but only one note.

There was more small laughter and chuckling, but Macklow, remembering the dowser, thinking about the new ripe garden and his own slow crops, would not laugh. Nor would Max with his new walking stick

One morning the man spoke to some people looking at his crop and studying what he had done to fix the house and the fence he had placed all around it. "I have hidden the music here. Music is a part of the soul. Music is part of the water too. And water is part of the soul.

Whoever finds the music I have hidden can have this house, for Macklow says it is mine to give."

Macklow nodded his head.

In the morning the man was gone. The tools were gone. The A-frame was gone.

People pored over the house trying to find the music. They did not know what they were looking for. But they found the dowser's well at the back end of the house and wondered at that. Macklow marveled at the well. However, he made sure none of them disturbed the things the man had done to fix the house.

It was curious. Nobody could find the music. None of them knew what they were looking for. But Max kept playing the whistle and kept hearing the note. He would sit on the porch and blow the whistle until people began to be bothered by it and asked him to stop.

But Max also knew that note deep inside his head.

For weeks people looked for the music. But they did not know what they were looking for.

And then, one morning as he walked past the house, Max hit one of the pickets with his stick.

Oh, how his heart pounded in his chest. How it grew it seemed that it might explode.

It was the same note from the whistle. The exact same, beautiful note.

Back to the gate he went, at the same note-sounding picket and began to walk around the house, his stick slapping against each picket in turn, the way boys have done ever since going by church and school yard fences.

And Macklow looked and the people looked and they all heard the music coming from the fence pickets as Max, walking without his stick support for the first time in his life, played elegant music on the ugly looking pickets with the stick the man had carved. The circled fence played out a whole lovely tune.

And Macklow saw to it that Max and his mother had themselves a new house to live in, at the place where the mountain comes to rest and the river is not yet found.

The Purple Sliver

Sasha, the 12-8 night cleaning woman, garrulous, bright, a nose for news, ostensibly done with her rounds for the midnight shift, set coffee for five and tea for one as the clock went past seven of the Monday morning. Windows and some properly-angled inner walls caught the dance of the early sun as it hustled into the suite, hastening the full day, the scurry or ambling of patients due for check-ups or the articulate knife of the surgeon and associated skills.

It was the last break of the shift for Sasha, tending the doctor, nurses, orderly and the receptionist of the dermatology surgical unit with an early treat, as they all gathered in an inner sanctum of the office proper, away from the patients soon to descend on them, her news of the night expected to headline the short session. There Sasha, the cleaning woman, was joined by Doctor Marjorie Aspermond, two nurses, Hillary Bent and Sue Gordon, Tyron Gaddis the orderly, and Michelle Aktiguan, the receptionist and computer operator, records keeper, filer of do's and don'ts, parking coordinator, etc. The entire unit well in place for over a year.

"You're gleaming, Sasha, absolutely gleaming!" injected Doctor Aspermond. "What's the news this time? Someone pregnant? Daughter getting married? Somebody steal the gold off the roof of the Statehouse?" Her own laughter was a guaranteed note of acceptance. She was herself infectious from Sasha's attitude, her stance on morning matters before the medical day imposed its demands, a break before business began its onset, its earnest retreat. A lovely early-morning beauty of the doctor's person gave her a bouncing claim of the day at hand; a well-coifed hair-do ready to be sacrificed to work, and otherwise slender and shapely all over from her delicate fingers to her fulsome and womanly presence. She was a knock-out in any crowd, an eye-grabber.

"Oh, Doc," Sasha said, tossing off "Doc" in early morning acceptance, pointing over her shoulder, "there was a shooting right up there on Charles Street last night, at the old brick church, glass shattered in some windows, two people dead. Harvey, the floor man on the first floor, talked to one of the cops who told him they were shot from outside, like hit or miss, and probably from long range, with a rifle, for certain he's thinking they were assassinated."

"Who got killed?" asked the doctor. "More than one killing attempted?"

"Harvey says he heard the two men killed stopped in every night, two men, big boys they are, shoulders like they're wearing Patriot shoulder pads, come by sort of late, say a few prayers, he'd guess, and go away on whatever rounds they had on their own calling," and she added an important note, "and they sat in the same pew every time. One of the deacons said so. And somebody else was there in the church, too, Harvey said, because the cops found a wet raincoat in the front row, like it had fallen there in the excitement and was forgotten, and no tags or labels on the raincoat and nothing in the pockets."

"Obviously someone who bolted from the church, didn't want to get shot or shot at. Didn't think for a second about his raincoat." The Doctor shrugged and asked, "They find his wallet or his calling card?"

They all laughed, the outside door closed again, a cough was heard, the kind that people use to announce their presence; day had begun for the second time.

After a minor surgery on an older man, rigid and humorless, and stitches removed from a curing patient, Doctor Aspermond looked at the chart of her third patient of the day, the surgery on his shoulder, fairly deep in her estimation and had required serious bandaging and protection against infection. Curtis Jenks was a local businessman who fronted for others, a charming talker, movie screen smile, handsome as the prince of the comics, and made a serious impression on others, bandaged or not. The curious attraction came to her in a hurry, was tolerated, hung around for a while ... until business made its persistent call.

"Well, Mr. Jenks, how's it feel today? Looks like that bandage slipped a little." Her touch at the bandage seemed to linger, which each party seemed to notice.

"Please," he said, "call me Curt, which stands for short and quick. It's easier that way. And you're right about that bandage. I felt a sharp pain yesterday, just like you said I would on the last visit. Quick and sharp and then gone, like an invitation to a party you don't want to go to." A solid, wide smile accompanied his statement.

She laughed respectably, looked closer at the bandage, her eyes noting a strangely foreign object within a portion of the gauze exterior, immediately held her breath back as she saw something she did not expect to see, and proceeded to take off the bandage, put it aside, and replaced it with new protection. On the side, away from the patient's view, she slipped a thin piece of glass she had found imbedded in the old bandage, a sliver with a purple tint to it, along with the old bandage, into a lab bag for testing. In her chest she felt her heart beating a little stronger, trying to prevent his seeing the motion, wondering if the heightened beating off her heart would send that message along to her hands and fingers, cut her short, fold up her day.

Undoubtedly, he had been exposed to some strange kind of impaction.

The slender piece of glass had penetrated the bandage and barely touched Jenks' wound or skin. The application of antibacterial ointment (a topical antibiotic) made him jump with a quick breath, from which he quickly settled back.

"Sorry about that," she said, patting him on the arm, but the beat of her heart still working its extra alarm.

"Hillary," she said in an unusually direct manner, "please re-bandage Mr. Jenks. I'll have the lab check the old one just in case." Turning to the patient, she said, "I'll see you in two weeks unless you get any new pains. Come see me immediately if you're in the area. I know you work locally, so you could manage it post haste. Michelle, out at the counter, will give you a new card for the next appointment. Please have a good day." She nodded with a deft and lovely movement that caught Jenks' eye the way some men note a manner of acceptance or wary inquisitiveness, interest being put into action, even if a mere announcement.

She left the surgical room and went to her office, her heart still pumping excitedly, momentarily feeling like she was Sasha at the grasp of a new headline, ready to broadcast her news to an attentive ear, a police ear, a dear friend at BPD headquarters.

"Frank Malmond," she said, trying to be calm, looking over her shoulder to make sure nobody else was in the room, ready to drop her voice an octave or two, keep "things" between friends. "Just tell him it's Marjorie from the hospital. He'll talk to me."

"Hello, Marjorie, this is a sudden pleasure. What can I do for you? Everything okay over your way?"

Gathering herself up, realizing doctor-patient confidence was working on her with quick little thrusts at her long beliefs, she said, "Frank, this is in strict confidence. No taping the message, no recording of any sort, and I want a solemn promise on it."

"I'll take care of it. Call me back at the other number. You know what it is."

His other phone rang and he said, "It's clean and clear now, Marjorie. Do you have a problem? You in trouble of any kind?"

"I won't give you a name, Frank, but I'll send you a lab bag from a patient I operated on perhaps a week ago or two. He walked in here today with a new pain that came about last evening." Her language was being carefully chosen, which both of them realized. There had been dozens, mostly minor excisions, a few extremely difficult ones; Jenks'd be in the big mix.

"I got that, and the implications. What'll I find in the bag ... besides the bandage?" She could picture him now standing beside his desk that she had seen but one time, long in the past, when her childhood classmate was first appointed to his current job, no more blue uniform for him, bound to rise in the ranks from the very beginning, as she had long believed.

"A sliver of glass, slightly colored, purplish, slender, not too long, but that the patient thought was a pain from the incision, perhaps an infection setting in. He thought it best to report the pain, so he walked in, not an appointment issue." The pause came in her voice, before she responded, "And he has no idea of what I found. Not the least. I took care of that."

"Marjorie," he said accidentally, "are you pointing at the church situation last night? Any reason to make that connection?"

She thought a while, could still see him standing at some kind of attention, not one to let any odd piece of information, any lead at all, slip past him. "It does sound odd, appear odd, and I know, from talk on the street, that someone else was in the church at the time the windows were shot in, smashed to smithereens, glass flying everywhere, like the fragmentation from shells and grenades you talked about one time. The police might have found his raincoat. Yes, glass fragmentation flying loose, one sliver finding roost." She could have laughed at the near rhyme in her voice, but held it back, not making it any sillier than it might really be. She had done her part, and not disclosed her patient's name.

"It's easy, Marjorie to issue a Subpoena Duces Tecum to get his records." He held back any further argument.

"I know that, Frank, but it gets so messy." She paused and added, "If it solves murder or throws some light on it, it's a fair trade. I can live with that between old classmates." She felt it was slightly twisted, but let it be. "All right, he works in the area as some kind of front man for big businesses, very confident type of guy, handsome as the day is long. His name is Curtis Jenks."

There, it was out, the office staff would not have to know anything about it. Her lab would not know. Sasha would never know, not from Frank Malmond, or the floor man, or the cop on the beat. The minute relaxation floundered in her, then found rest.

And at the other end of the phone, as he hung it up, admiring Marjorie's stance, her initial beliefs, her social and medical responsibilities, he breathed a sigh of relief: Curtis Jenks' participation in this matter would have shaken Marjorie all the more: he was none other than Frank Malmond's personal undercover man from BPD, a hidden entity from most regular knowledge down through the ranks as the best undercover BPD agent on the force, in the city, still unknown to the mob at large, to all criminal conglomerates, and to the general public.

Tonight they'd sit in a booth at the Port Hole Pub in Lynn, sly, secretive as possible, garbed in heavier work clothes, generally appearing only on late Saturday evenings, friendly with both the waiter and the bartender, and walking out apparently drunk or teetering noisily at the end of their evening, but sober as truant officers.

Their conversation, somewhat illuminating to each one, and what would have shaken up Doctor Marjorie Aspermond for a whole weekend, went like this:

Curtis Jenks: I waited in the church for them. They always manage to meet there between 7 and 8 on Friday evenings, make a show of it, whisper like we do now, slip parcels to each other, once a German automatic I saw plain as day in a plastic bag so no fingerprints were left on it, or the ones that were there were preserved for other eyes. I was there the first time they came in, and they gawked around like first-time visitors. It was accidental providence that I spotted them in the church at that time, and recognized them from Winter Hill. They didn't pay any attention to me after that first session. I don't know where that was going on with them, but it's obvious, from what happened, that someone else knew there'd be there."

Frank Malmond; Something else here? You got that look on your face.

Curtis Jenks: The best part, the best and only lead before I ducked out, came between the first shot smashing a big window and the second shot smashing the second window. That's when I saw a light go out in the tallest building off the northeast corner, the Christopher's Founders Building with the huge cross lit up on top, tall as Bunker Hill Monument. On the top floor, and in the farthest corner window, a light went out like it had been shut off at the snap of a trigger or a finger. Bingo! Job done, even from that distance. And I bolted out of the church by the side door.

Frank Malmond: Like a second person was on site, up there at the Christopher's?

Jenks: Yup, right to a tee.

Malmond: You sure about that location?

Jenks: Sure as shooting. I went over there after my flight from the church, not caring to be an accident at an assassination. I brought a flashlight, a couple of dust clothes, my super glass, a few plastic bags to hold possible evidence.

Malmond: Get any?

Jenks: Gunpowder from a window ledge, and my camera for fingerprints on the scene, perhaps 50 of them, but some of them are classical impressions fresh as a daisy in bloom. The can't miss type. And on top of a baseboard heater, merged against the wall, I found an empty rifle shell, a 30-06 Springfield. They'll all be in the lab today. Sounds like you had an early and ready grasp on this situation? Like you had someone there at the church or nearby?

Malmond: A friendly tip.

Jenks: The only one it can be then is the doc who worked on me, a knockout from the first word, but I find it hard to believe she gave me up.

Malmond: She didn't give you up because I twisted her right up front with a Subpoena Duces Tecum. It was fair and square from where I sit.

In a matter of a day's examination, fingerprints were traced, the rifle found, the shell proven to have been fired from the Springfield, dubbed "the sniper's rifle" of preference through many of our wars.

On his return trip to see Doctor Marjorie Aspermond, excuses and forgiveness were readily acknowledged and accepted, and when he turned at the door to look back at her, she said, "Don't go yet, Curt. There's someone here that would like to have dinner with you some night."

Jenks, with a half-smile, nodded his head as he stood at the door, just as she added, "Like tonight? We're already involved."

Lavery Tells It All

I'm a cop from Saxon, name of Sigmund Lavery. My wife Alicia says I'm retired, but as long as I breathe, I'll be a cop. I've locked up a ton of wild ones and sly ones and rapacious ones. You name them, I've grabbed them. And a lot of them have been odd cases from the very start, then things seemed to slow down, and things went well, and the outlook on crime and its habituals swung through a slight change.

Not that they were tolerated changes, but some days it took too long to get going on corrective action.

So we get to the story at hand. Somewhere along the line things had got out of hand; graves were being robbed at Riverbend Cemetery, sitting just above Shallow Brook on a flat area that's been flooded over a couple of times in its history. Stealing coins, too, strange as it seems. That's the kind of thing can yank a town right off its feet, drop it to its knees, even if the spread of the cemetery is closing fast on its capacity and a brand new site is coming soon under "new business."

That's going to be hot before it cools off.

From my perspective, I figure it all started more than 70 years earlier, my being an old time Saxonian and a long-time cop. That's when Mr. Trinidad, on the side of a steep rise on Hill Street, began placing coins into the wet cement of new steps rising from the street, 82 steps in all, to his front door. Never any gold coins there in that cement, never precious ones or collectibles, but mostly copper pennies and now-and-then silver coins knurled on the edge, all becoming midnight targets for us four kids of the neighborhood as tight as a Billy Conn fist or even Joe Louis's.

We'd bring our small hammers and little cold chisels thin as scalpels and tap away near Friday midnights for coins for our State Theater visits on Saturday where waiting for us were The Lone Ranger or Flash Gordon or Buck Jones, each of them practically calling us by name. We slipped out of bedroom windows for the thievery, silent as nighthawks or footpads or other prowlers, and I bet you can just see us on the way up those steps on a dark Friday night and into the theater on a bright Saturday afternoon, the line of kids waiting to buy tickets wound around the side of the theater and down along the railroad tracks.

Often I thought that Mr. Trinidad sat on his porch listening to us, like we were miners, giggling at clumsy thefts, enjoying the cheap comedy. Oh, there'd be small curses and pinched fingers aplenty among us, and knees that cement left bruised and memorable. Only recently it occurred to me that he was henchman and plotter along with us. Kind of a reverse gear Santa Claus. On good days we knew he sat there looking out over the river and we could smell his coffee, but never once catching a real shadow of him.

Now, a whole half century later, someone's robbing graves at Riverbend Cemetery, and stealing coins, among other items left in memory, for memory or, occasionally, one still begging for mercy for some old nastiness. A few of those coins had been set into small cement additions coupled onto the stone bases (Oh, we had some hard labor artists in our town) and these had been chipped away from their eternal banks. Probably with little hammers and cold chisels, clinks and pings never heard, but someone, I figured, who knew about the Mr. Trinidad's steps, the inlaid treasure trove of our younger days.

Dirk Edwards, one of us tight-as-wad four, out of a long and imposing silence since his son's death, had come to the police station, yelling at old Chief Sherbrook. "I leave coins on my son's grave. He spent his days collecting coins. Every time I find something he never had, I leave it on the base of his stone. Not for long, but to let him know I'm thinking of him. Now, someone's robbing him!"

He was a big man, deeply browed, and his arms loomed like separate chassis coming out of a short sleeve shirt. Anger hid just out of sight when it came to Dirk. Anger could have been easy with him. "I just leave them on the rim of the stone. Now I'm going to put them down with goddamned epoxy, you can bet your sweet ass on that. Son of a bitch, I'll kill the guy I ever catch him!" Down the steps of the station he went, gargantuan, head big as a beehive, splashy red suspenders tight on that massive chest, his fists hard against pants pockets. He'd just finished talking more than he had talked in the whole damned sorrowful, sad, pitiful year.

But he hadn't cried yet. I was worried about the time when he would cry.

Not a chance his ever being the brightest apple in the barrel, old Dirk, but he'd been one of us. Early on we had noticed he always squinted his eyebrows at every part of a conversation going on around him, as though he was measuring each word said, each thought proffered, and a really deep measurement at that. It took us some time to realize that behind his dark brown eyes was a space like a huge garage or barn that had gone out of business, and all the stalls were empty. In most of those conversations, he kept quiet, nodding, squinting, and being himself. Of course, we never really got to know him. Silence takes some people away from normal perception, and into strange sanctuaries. But he'd been one of our boyhood chippers, one of our pals, though time had long since dropped its long and dark veil between us.

I was wondering how deep that old bond would find itself these days, lots of spilt milk along the way.

The runner, Mary Applegate, came the very next day to the station, her voice raucous and strident coming out of such a slight, thin frame. To me she was mostly a stranger in town, nothing other than a slim shadow in local road races, an apparition loping alongside the Saxon River.

"They're grave robbers! Nothing but grave robbers! I want that known!" Oh, that slim, shadowy lady had a voice loud as the steam whistle at the GE.

A fifty-year old school teacher, she had retired early, and was now given to running long distance races. Her twin sister was buried at Riverbend after a horrible accident, and Mary had spent the better part of three years in the cemetery, morose, clinging to the old days, a bag of woes. Running, initially away from her problems, had given her a new liberty, a new outlook. But her little gifts left for her sister Margaret were being stolen in the night. They were simple things, like Margaret's first harmonica found in the attic, an old collection of Quaker Oats paper dolls wrapped in Cellophane or Saran wrap, a white-metal penny from World War II, a small but highly understood page from a dance book three times holding the name of a boy who never came home from some place called Burma in WW II, things that made Mary ache all over again. "I want the police down there every night!" Truth is, Mary knew a couple of cops met their quick dates in the dark cemetery, midnight or later, but decided to leave well enough alone. Some of the cops wore stripes. Some of the ladies she knew. Some of them had been students of hers. Now they were studying law.

The new police chief was an old patrolman who had slowly and methodically climbed the ranks, like a mountain climber learning on the job, at The Matterhorn or K-27 itself, a long haul. His name was Tutor Sherbrook and at a rather boisterous meeting with some of the victims he promised, "I'll have a patrol car in there a few times every night. No schedule, just a random kind of visit, so as not to frighten away the thief until he's in our sights. That place is going to be full up before we know it."

I remember just about every word uttered at that meeting, from every speaker.

Tutor Sherbrook's old patrolman's eyes, long used to measuring intensity or danger or doubt or facial incredulity, scanned the audience. His round face had a big mouth, bigger ears, and a nose once clubbed into near submission in a small riot. He had no trouble in being unpleasant.

Clinton Motherwell was surprised at the dictate. Clint, like Dirk, was one of the old four. "Chief," he said, "I don't doubt that you mean well. You got our respect." Everybody in the room knew he was saying, "Even if you are slow as hell in most things, we respect your determination."

After the modulated pause, Clint continued, "Never has been a sighting. Never has been a single light seen in the cemetery to show this crud where he's going, what he's at. Does that strike you as odd, Chief? I mean, real odd, or really not odd at all?" He looked around as though answers had already popped up.

"Just says he's real careful, to me. Maybe uses one of them pocket kind of flashlights. Could be a number of things." The chief leaned toward the audience, which Clint knew was one of his crude assumptions of position.

Clint waved one hand and bounced it off the side of his head in subtle exasperation. "Ever think, Chief, that we won't get a look at him at night at all, because he goes in there during the day and sees everything he needs to see and knows exactly where to go in the dark. Without benefit of a damned flashlight. Or not a single match struck in his whole outing. Plots his time and target, he does, right under everybody's eyes."

"What you're saying, Clint, is that he could be one of us in this room right now."

"Aha," I said to myself, thinking Alicia ought to see me in action now, because something was breaking loose right in our midst and I was still in the mix.

"You're damn right," Clint threw back at him. "Could be any one of us. We've all seen what the hell kind of stuff has been ending up as mementos, and all the time the character of the cemetery, right under our noses, has been changing. That's not news to any of us. The town is changing. Old, sedate Riverbend is no longer sedate. It's about had its day and we better face that sooner than we thought."

Mary Applegate came right up out of her seat, her voice reaching the rafters. "What do you mean, the character of the cemetery has been changing? I think that's ridiculous. My sister is there. It's the only place left for me to visit her. What are you talking about character for? I think it's crude and gruesome."

Clint was not offended, but you could tell he was ready for her. "Mary, just hear me out. Have you noticed what has happened lately in the cemetery around Halloween time? Just in the last couple of years?"

"Of course, I have," Mary said, the look on her face saying she thought Clint wouldn't believe she had an answer. "That's when the pumpkins started showing up. I think it's beautiful. It's a lovely expression of a time that might go unnoticed in the cemetery, if it wasn't for some thoughtful individuals."

"Let me tell you what happened, Mary," Clint said. "One day I'm down at the cemetery, a couple of days before Halloween, and I come on my parents' stone and I see a beautiful pumpkin right on their grave. Nothing carved, no face, just a healthy pumpkin, and a decent-sized one to boot. In the whole cemetery, just that one pumpkin. One pumpkin! At supper that night, right at the table, I mentioned how nice it was seeing the pumpkin there. I said it had given me goose bumps and I thought perhaps my cousin Emily had put it there because she highly favored my mother who made Halloween very special for us.”

His pause was a serious one, as though it was getting loaded with a final round. “My daughter coughed, and looked at me with her thirteen-year old eyes kind of shaded and said, ‘It wasn’t Em, Dad, it was me.’ So I asked her where she got the pumpkin and she looked me square in the eyes again and said, ‘You don’t want to know, Dad.’ Just like that and he snapped his fingers. “I knew she had swiped it off someone’s front steps. It was the thought that counted, not the gesture. A week later there must have been a hundred pumpkins down there.”

“What the heck are you trying to say, Clint?” Mary was shrugging her shoulders and looking around at everybody. What she was broadcasting was the thought that Clint was different than the rest of them. He wrote poems, didn’t he? They all knew that. “Give us poor folk a clue, Clint.” The thin runner’s frame was upright in the aisle, like a sign pole at a bus stop.

“I’m saying whoever is doing this stealing has a different agenda in mind. He has another purpose in mind.” Clint Motherwell looked around to see if any of it had sunk in. He was thinking it might be the argument about the new cemetery.

Mary finally broke free of herself. “You poets sure have a strange way of saying things, and stranger ideas. What are you talking about? I swear, Clinton Motherwell, you throw me right off my stride.” She shrugged her shoulders again in the universal gesture.

Chief Tutor Sherbrook was nodding at Clint. “You mean the group who’s trying to close up Riverbend sooner than later and start another cemetery someplace else, like in Harry Garvey’s property, also over against the Saxon River? Harry’s not been out of the house in a year or more. Never goes to the cemetery, though his Wilma’s there. It sure isn’t him. How would this thieving help in that regard, being three sites under discussion? Looks like a dead-ender to me.” His stern look swept over the crowd. “Nothing new here but some swift objections and more noise. You know what I’m going to do about this mess, and all I ask is that all of you keep your eyes open.”

Two mornings later the cruiser passing through the cemetery came across two dozen stones smashed into ungainly pieces, sharp as ax heads. The word spread around town and a hundred people gathered at the cemetery. The chief came down with a couple of sergeants. One stone belonged to Margaret Applegate, Mary’s sister. Another stone was that of Dirk Edwards’ son, Anthony. The method of damage looked purposeful, loaded with direction, intent, malice.

The next morning there were two dead dogs and a dead cat right in the middle of the Veterans Section. Nearly the whole town went ballistic. There were meetings at the VFW and the American Legion and at the DAV. The State Police received a call, anonymous of course.

Clint was pretty damn certain there was a hidden reason behind the whole situation at Riverbend. He came by the house the next evening. "I've got to talk to someone about this, Sig. Nobody stealing pennies or nickels or dimes, like we used to do at Mr. Trinidad' steps, wants to get rich. Shoot, we only went to see the movies, cowboy films mostly, Roy or Gene or Hoppy getting more bowlegged all the time. We didn't even realize they never kissed a girl. All that was beyond us. And who the hell out there wants an old harmonica or goddamn paper dolls even if they are collectibles? Or Syd Welling's out-of-tune trumpet for God's sake? Old Syd never finished a tune in his whole life. He couldn't carry a note in a briefcase. Something else is going on here. I can feel it in my bones."

I didn't really know what Clint was getting at, but I knew this much: that whatever idea he had, whatever lurked in the back of his mind, and I was sure that something had cemented itself there, Clinton Motherwell wanted that idea to come out of my mouth and not his. He wanted me to be aware of it, as if it were first-hand with me. It was now painfully obvious to me that he had a severe suspicion of someone in town. All his life Clint had worked that way. And he was good at it. I had never undertaken a study to find out why. It was just his modus operandi. I knew I had to watch carefully as the whole thing might unravel itself, right there in front of me.

We pitched ideas back and forth and nothing spectacular or seemingly possible came out of the dialogue. Then, in one sweep, Clint made a move. He said, "Do you have one of those maps of the town that the Bicentennial Committee had printed?"

"The one with all the businesses and municipal locations shown? The green map?"

"Yah," Clint said, "that's the one, Sig." Damn, I could see something in his eye, the way he so offhandedly said, "Yah."

I got a copy from the den and laid it out on the kitchen table. Everything that was anything in the way of business or municipal was shown. That included cottage industry stuff and home quarters for landscapers and whatever you could name. They all had paid a piece of the cost in getting the map done. It said money all over it. I kept thinking about something I read about writers and readers and books; "Everything comes right back to money and sex. That's what writers write, what readers read, what moneymakers look for as they hang out in every corner of creation. Even in literature. Crime books. Comic books. They all have the good guys and the bad guys. The good girls and the bad girls. And money and sex, good or bad, is always at one end or the other."

I don't think I made a dent at all in Clint's thinking; something was cemented there already.

He leaned over my map, studying it, but I noticed his eyes almost involuntarily zipping back at the Garvey property, near the Saxon River, where some people said a new cemetery should be located. His eyes were like the platen on a typewriter, going back to the beginning all the time. There was room enough at Garvey's for a new cemetery, though it was only one of three sites that came up in discussions. He started pointing out places that I knew as well as he did. I was sure he was being coy about his suspicions to the very end… that would be my saying, with some kind of start like … "What about this, Sig?"

And there it was, what he was trying to get me to say, smack dab at one end of the Garvey property, Beau LeBlanc's florist shop and nursery. Beau had also been one of us four for the movies. And right there I knew that Clint knew. He knew what I knew, that Beau had the mind and the attitude to do what had been done at Riverbend to try to get the new cemetery near his place of business. He'd be way ahead of the other florists if he did. He'd always managed to come out on top, by any means he could. And I suddenly heard his voice, all those years in the past, saying one dark evening as we sat in Ollie Caldwell's field watching the fireflies, "I think we ought to get a hammer and chisel some night and get some money from old man Trinidad's steps. He probably sleeps all night long and wouldn't even hear us."

Three nights later, after Clint's visit, they caught Beau LeBlanc stuffing toy mementos and pictures left for the dead into an old gunnysack. In the trunk of his car they found a ball peen hammer, an eight-pounder he had probably used to smash the memorial stones at the cemetery, and some of Dirk Edmund's coins were cached in a small leather pouch. They found Margaret Applegate's old harmonica and some other doo-dads Mary had left. Beau went that one step beyond, like the old days, figuring how to get Mr. Trinidad's coins free of cement.

After lots of noise and Dirk almost beating the hell out of his old boyhood pal, and Mary instituting a suit against Beau, the town selected a new site for the new cemetery. It was not near the Saxon River, and not near Beau LeBlanc's Gay Parisian Nursery. And none of his thousand hours of imposed community service could be performed anywhere near the cemetery, new or old.

Incendiary at Odds

Dock Hobson, PI extraordinaire and a man of diverse talents, was two houses away, in the attic, in free space without a hit on his budget because it was the house of an old teacher of his, had the volume set at mid-range to the pipe he had set into the other house more than 17 months earlier. Perhaps all that dirty work on his part, the ultimate in sneaking, in artful patience, was going to pay off in spades. The words were coming in as clear as a Sony mike. He'd sure use them for motivation.

There was a moment of self-admiration for his foresight, his planning and the patience of the ages that sat inside him, part and parcel of his soul.

For more than those 17 months, he had been snaking his way along in life with Chuck and Jumbo. He owed them as others did, he was sure, owed them, all the way owed them. Either Chuck Duckworth or Jumbo Laverty, or both, had hit his secretary Bunny Duval, the most hidden woman he had ever known, and the clear love of his life, the one most missed for sure. They had dropped her off her balcony with two silenced rounds.

The why was never announced, never came off even in ink, nobody uptown or downtown saying one damned word, which they had often done to jerk his chain, nor no masked call on his phone saying reparation had been accomplished. But he knew Chuck and Jumbo had gone extra-curricular.

Working outside the bounds, beyond the chain markers, making points, kissing ass. That kind of stuff usually didn't pay, not in the end. They'd come some payback, he knew, just like he knew The Our Father to the last breath in the last word.

Her body, over the rail in free fall, hit the cement walk the way grumpy old ironworkers say the stop is sudden, sudden and conclusive. And bloody awful, to boot. The police had recovered a single expended shell casing, with no fingerprints, in a nearby apartment of a guy who had won a trip to Disneyworld. Hobson had been checking "that fix" too, but so many loose ends made it like a live wire in a puddled street. Nothing had been nailed down in that direction. Not a whisper. Not a phony tip, the way tipsters try to keep all four lanes open, the alleys clean of deadwood pins.

Hobson, almost giddy at times, fed himself with images that leaped up from all his past observations of the pair, from close range as well as under a Palomar-strong telescope. He knew them like characters in the final act of a play coming to an end, the curtain ready to drop, the resolution about to happen, hope or demise on the threshold. Or an old black and white movie where he could recite the dialogue like he was reading a strip of text. Dick Powell without a song on his lips. Humphrey Bogart at his best cowing a whole ensemble of other hard characters. Chester Morris, as Boston Blackie, clearly tailing a suspect in the darkness.

Chuck Duckworth, in the cellar of the house where they kept their guns, had complained generally about the new hit they were to get paid for. In most things he was dumb as mud, Jumbo Laverty was thinking, but he never missed what he shot at … turkeys, wild boars, deer, all up-country or, down here in the city, a contract hit silhouetted behind a shade, shadowy in a window, sitting on a lonely bench in the park feeding the stupid pigeons.

"Blow it out your ass, Chuck," Laverty said, "it ain't counting here. Complain all you want, but a job's a job. You knew that when you signed on. We don't do it no other way, 'cepting something different like The Man says."

He patted the .38 Special sitting in the shoulder holster as if it was a toy. "But we got to get more inventive here. That's what The Man keeps saying. He says too many fingerprints come off of guns, shell casings, et cet like they say down home. So, we gotta think about a new way of knocking this guy for the count; 1-2-3 you're gonzo, baby. It's just a job we're doing, and nothing personal. If only all those dead suckers know, it's just a job."

Duckworth, brothel-groping an Uzi, thumb working like it was on a lifted, stove-pipe nipple, getting nervous and excited all at the same time while sitting in a hard-back chair, said, "You talk like it's Murder Inc. It's just an everyday hit on a damned asshole what's screwing things up for the whole city. No big deal in that, just like you figure it. We could pump him once or twice, lead or juice. Let him bleed or get hooked on the juice. Make his whole friggin' crowd sweat out their ass." Then, thinking it all out a little more, looking for something hard, real, said, "What's his name? You ain't told me yet."

"Chuck, you got to be the dumbest shit I ever knew. No names. Never say a name no matter what. No matter where you are. I don't care if you're thinking to yourself, if you could, don't say no names. People are always listening to what's being said. Don't let one word, or one hit's name, hang you or get the friggin' chair for you. It ain't worth it."

The pause he let hang out spelled it all: "I don't get to even see The Man myself, not really face to face. I talk to him through a screen, a dark mesh screen, him on the other side."

"It sounds like a damn confessional. You gotta say, 'Forgive me, Father, for I have sinned?'"

"Don't be no shithead on me, though it's like that, almost. He don't trust nobody, way I look at it. And he came after me. I didn't go after him," and the balance came out like the lyrics in the song, "and then there was you."

Duckworth laughed and then said, "Can we say the place? Hell, we're in the dark almost down here. Nobody knows nuts about this place."

"Chuck, you don't listen none to me. No names. No nouns. No nothing, but we got a job. A new payday's coming." The music was back in his voice.

"Good," Duckworth said, "I might need a new suit."

"What the hell do you need a new suit for? Never even seen you in an old suit."

Duckworth snickered loudly, like the mike was down in his throat, nuzzling his diaphragm. "I was thinking," he said with some joyous deliberation, "I'd maybe go to the hit's funeral."

Hobson jerked backwards with a start when Jumbo Laverty leaped into the air in front of him. "Don't be a shithead, Chuck. I swear you'll be the death of me yet. Clues will kill us too. You got to keep remembering that. No clues. No clues ever. No free-for-the-taking profiles like on them TV movies."

Hobson measured the ensuing silence, Duckworth admonished, Laverty deep in thought. He could see the pair of them. "I ought to write plays," he said to himself as the silence continued and he saw his characters in a mindful study, their moves in a kind of slow motion gait but center stage every minute.

It was Duckworth who broke the silence. "Know what I was just thinking about, Jumbo? This gas crunch. I saw a Jeep go by the other day and with two GI gas cans strapped on the rear end like we had in the army, the 5-gallon kind, but these were chained and locked, the guy ascared they're going to be swiped or siphoned off. Had friggin' chains right over the top of them, gas near $5.00 a gallon'll do that.

There was more silence, then Duckworth said, "What if we pour gas all over the outside of the place at night, soak down the doorways, set it off from a car or from down the street, like a flipped butt or a cigar, and just keep riding or walking. That place'd burn like a Roman friggin' candle, chances it's so old and dusty. Pop goes the weasel and it'd be gone up in smoke and neighbors a mile away would find their gutters jammed with leaves all on fire. It'd be friggin' electric."

His pause was also deliberate, like added punctuation. "Just like this place. A guy wants us, soaks it, we ain't got a friggin' chance. Poof goes Puff the Magic Dragon."

Jumbo Laverty, suddenly awake at the other end of the pipe, said, "That's inventive, I got to say, Chuck. No guns with no prints and no old bullet casings. I'll ask The Man what he thinks."

"Can I go with you?"

"Nobody talks to The Man but me, the same way as always, like a one-way street almost."

Hobson, more than four years' work floating in his mind, knowing he had never successfully tailed Jumbo Laverty, who was as alert as any perp he had ever tailed, knew he had to stay put again, at the end of the pipe, in an old teacher's house, the space for free for a few old-time favors if he could stomach it any more, her age really catching up with his appetite. He checked the fridge, the small stock of crackers, chips, Doritos, his tongue at remembering. Oh, the memories. For a bare instance he tasted Bunny, remembered a favorite pose, saw her waiting in that pose, then watched her quickly disappear.

He'd stay to the end. He'd stay for Bunny and justice, one way or the other. All the perps in the world couldn't match up to her.

Laverty, he knew, would leave the other house and space himself out in two or more hours of sly movement until his scheduled meeting with The Man.

That irony swelled in him like a batch of yeast-ridden dough in an old pan.

He'd let Jumbo go his way and sit by while he waited for Chuck Duckworth to shoot off his mouth. Now and then, over the long haul, old Duckworth would oblige him. "Dumb as mud," Laverty had said, and he was right smack on the nail head.

Hobson saw both hitters in a variety of poses, like they were shining up to a photographer.

Duckworth was always ready with a shit-eating grin like he'd just beat his bookie out of a grand or two and all he owed on his tab. Laverty, on the other hand, played it like an old Hollywood bit player, a character actor, a support man like Paul Fix, Noah Beery, Jr., doing just enough to get through the scene, do his professional bit, take his pay, and bow out until the next scene came along. Quick images rushed him, like Jim Brown coming off-tackle on the old slant play, and he saw Walter Brennan and Walter Huston and Roscoe Karns in black and white glory. Laverty and Duckworth were different, and that was to his advantage. With Bunny sitting in the wings waiting for payback.

His sixth sense set him up; he could feel it coming. Duckworth had been in absolute silence for well over an hour after Laverty had left, except for a cough or two, one sneeze, and then, finally, a click. A solid give-away click; Duckworth had picked up the phone, dialed a number, heard the reverse clicking away, paused, heard a female voice, sweet, delicious, dripping, like it was a house full of her sisters, say, "Is that you, sweetbread? Where you been? You on another stake-out? Don't the 'partment ever give you a break?"

"Hon, you wear the badge, you take the breaks. It's in the blood."

"I know what's in your blood, sweetbread, and where it likes to spend its time. When do I get to see you? I'm getting there in an awful hurry every night now, all on my own."

"We have a big one now, watching a big bookie what ain't a big bookie, if you get my drift. But he's got the numbers right, way I see it."

"Sweetbread," she said, "you're always full up with mystery, but you ain't answered me yet… when do I get to see you?"

"I can tell from my partner that we're closing in on the big one. Might take me a week, maybe less, but the payday is big and I'm promising a week at Disney or wherever wings can take us. You free to travel, I'd bet?"

"What you up to, sweetbread, so full of mystery and staying away from me. That's not fair. How long you gonna be away?"

Turkey Fulture, at The Man's orders, sat on a rickety chair on a nearby rooftop, an old Ought-Three GI issue sniper rifle, a Springfield with silencer, in his hands. He looked the assassin type. Thin composite of anger and pure hatred. His childhood on full display. His eyes shining like embers in the thinning daylight. Waiting like he was in a hunter's blind. (Huh! Fucking dumb deer deserved it every time out; stupid is as stupid does.) Commission money was at hand. A piece-of-cake job. A couple of rounds point blank (like he could miss anything!!), drop the clean weapon, scatter his way out of there, no trace on the lip of anything. Done and gone. He had done it close to 50 times. The real count would come to him, the exact count, when he was paid off, when he arrived at the cabin deep in Maine woods, got his boots, hit the stream, let life carry him away for a solid week of nothing but chucking brookies and bigger stuff up on the banking.

He fired at the gas can one of the men was carrying and it blew up in a lightning burst, the three new assassination candidates gone in a searing flash and some unhealthy screams. The fire ran around the whole building like it was an arrow out of a hot quiver, a hot spot if there ever was one. With a roar the flames shot up the sides of the building, yanked clapboards loose of nails like popcorn on the run, smashed windows, made entries as common as late-night break-ins. A woman screamed down the street. A child answered. Someone yelled, "Fire! Fire! Fire!"

"That clears the ticket for The Man," Turkey said, his voice soft and clear as he moved back to the door to the stairs. He'd be out of there in the matter of minutes, down three flights of darkness, into an alley of darkness, into the subway system, swing around the horn a few times, disappear for a few weeks in Maine going after those tiny brook trout smothered in cornmeal and butter. And beer for breakfast! He could taste the beer for breakfast. He'd make that happen every day he was deep in the woods.

The shot from the rooftop doorway hit Turkey directly in the forehead and splattered his brains like pigeon shit. The Ought 3 fell away from Turkey's gloved hands. The Man said Laverty or Duckworth had last handled it, only the day before. "Let the cops screw with that one," Turkey had muttered to no one in particular at that time.

The final shooter, who had shot Turkey from about eight feet away, taking him out of the loop, was only three steps down the stairs when the bomb under his feet went off.

Across the street, in another apartment, The Man marked events, heard gunfire, saw the explosion, counted all the witnesses having gone down the drain.

He went back to the pipe, disconnected the wires, packed it all away in a trash bag, dumped it, in the dark, in a dumpster way up-town, then lit it up, "A bonfire for Bunny," he muttered, walking away and looking back once, liking fire since he was a kid, using it.

The Kelly Green Colt

Leland Stanford, great horse ranch owner in California, once sent his foreman, Sam Lindsey, to find the true story of Cavan, a Kelly green colt he heard had been stolen. Said the colt owner, "Little tracks are all about, tracks of little people with little shoes. They're all around the barn and the fences and lead off to the pasture and the far gate. I tried to trail them, but they withered away. Even the tracks of Cavan and his dam Bogger, just disappeared, as if in one stride, as if they had not been there at all."

"Or here," he admonished.

Lindsey visited hundreds of ranches inquiring about Cavan, the Kelly green colt, and the black dam Bogger, apparently taken away by the little people. At length his children and grandchildren inherited a famous horse ranch that grew to encompass lands on both sides of the Mississippi and up through the northern territories.

And so, a few years later, Lindsey's five-year-old grandson, having heard the stories about the Kelly green colt, was visiting a Kansas fairgrounds. He tried to pull his father away from a hotdog vendor. "I saw my pony!" he yelled, and kept yelling as his father was trying buy two hotdogs, "I saw my pony! I saw my pony!"

His father, hands full, finally said, "What pony, Cavan?" He looked at the vendor, shrugged his shoulders, each smiling at the boy.

"My green pony," he said, "the one mom and grandma always told me about." He pointed across the fairgrounds to the merry-go-round where, in circular and continuous path, a Kelly green pony rushed in circles and leapt high and low, and the sun shone on it like a green gem.

Then the boy pointed at little footprints on the ground.

The Melatonic Aftermath

It was evident my boss and his boss, and whoever were ass-kissers further up the line, had it in for me. The note was on my desk on Monday morning when I got to work usually more than an hour early to wind myself up for the day: Effective this date, you are hereby transferred to our West Coast facility at San Diego. Air transportation has been arranged and tickets and data are available at the Cashier's Office. There was no signature, but it was official paper, and not a practical joke.

If you knew me there, in all my years, you knew I'd not go peeking around for answers, seeking reasons, responsible souls brought face to face. Do and get done, I'd always said, even to my boss, who never had a response but a weak smile, if you can call that a retort. That was the essence of his imagination.

I got my tickets and travel info ... and walked out. I had three days to nestle down elsewhere, where I'd never been. No sense hanging around here where I was not wanted, so I got elsewhere in all haste.

Nobody greeted me. Not a soul. I walked in, walked around, waited to see my name on a door, a hand reach out to welcome or congratulate me ... nothing, no one, NO BODY like the commercial says.

Three days later I was still wandering, getting lunch for free, but no discussions with anybody. I was willing to wait it out, just to make my own statement.

Finally, one guy in work clothes said to me in the chow line, "I know you're new here, but don't know where your office is, or even if you have one. What's your title? I make signs here and get things done. I try to stay ahead of the game, which gets a bit fuzzy at times."

"I'm the new Director of Shitting and Crapping."

"Okay," he said, "I'll have a sign made for you." There was no pussyfooting around from him.

I said, "Where will you hang it?"

"That's easy," he said, "on your office door."

"Where's that?"

"I'll arrange that for you, and furnish it too. That's part of my job here."

"I like the way you work."

"Good. Look for changes in the morning. My crew works fast."

In the morning I found my office, with a computer right smack dead center on my desk. It was a beauty. A note attached to it said, in a smooth hand, "Your usage password is D of S&C."

I studied the situation from my desk, all that had transpired, and wrote my first declaration:

As of this moment, all rest rooms will be used only on Thursdays. No other day is allowed for shitting or crapping. We have ordered 7000 feet of waste pipe to be used in a major remodeling effort, but delivery is delayed until Friday this week, so the effort will begin on the weekend. (Signed) Director of S&C.

Only 20 minutes later my lone pal in denim stuck his head into my office and said, "Hope you're comfortable, but I have to tell you that maintenance work cannot, by contract, be accomplished on the weekend, so it will not ensue until Monday morning at 7:00 A.M. sharp." He tipped his work cap to me and left.

I left my office at 4:30 P.M., saw all restrooms banded with yellow tape and a prominent door sign saying, in a very neat hand, Closed until further notice, per the Director of S&C. Maintenance work on this site will proceed on Monday A.M.

When I popped the beeper on my rental car, I heard the door latches click in a kind of musical arrangement, making me feel in sync with all matters, the good feeling for the first time in a long time surge down through me so heavily it looked for a breakout. It went off in a scream of "Yayuh" that I'm sure reached the end of the parking lot. Some folks looked at me, a few oddly, a few suspecting pleasure was in their midst, one or two guys still sour about a sunrise "NOT NOW!"

I looked a few of the good ones in the eyes, smiled as wide as a billboard and yelled, "Why the hell not. I'm going up to the mountains and get some fresh air." One guy threw his hands in the air as if I had just scored a touchdown. His counterpart, perhaps an old baseball ump, gave off the "safe" sign, his arms as level as the tarmac under us.

Another thought leaped free as those mountains, as I knew I was free of S&C but still in sync, all in the midst of joy at tumult.

For hours, without drinking or eating and only one gas stop, I stepped out on top of a mountain; I almost let the gorgeous wind blow me away. I didn't give a crap about anything --- here or there.

A woman, thin and delicious looking without the roll, said, "What else is on your mind?" She was blasphemously beautiful.

"I'm at that critical juncture in my life where it has to go off by itself, because I'd marry you in a minute and we'd be happy for life but you'd have to go back to Boston with me."

I told her the whole story. She kept laughing and smiling and let loose with a joyous tickle in her throat time and time again, grabbed my hand, pulled me close and said, "Let's go back to my room for the pre-nuptials."

She had hooked me deeply. She sat atop me making awed sweet-sweat demands, to my relenting pleasure.

The captain of the plane married us hastily after a concentrated urging, I left her at my old apartment and then I went to see my old boss.

"Where the hell have you been, Jack? Someone said you went on a hunting trip. I didn't know you were a hunter, but regardless, I've got good news for you. The CEO at our West Coast facility has resigned due to some rigmarole or mix up and you got the job if you want it. Know anybody out there to get a head start on things?"

I almost pissed my pants when he said "head start."

Watchdog with a Pretty Face

Seventy years old, a widow for 10 years but not really showing her age, Agnes Stanvyck remembered her Girl Scout days filled with preparation, alertness, compassion, and now they played a continuous role in her living alone. Coming into her life at this lonely period was a sense of disturbance at one of her neighbors whose actions bothered her from first notice. George Thresher stood again inside his garage, the sliding door flung open, with a pair of binoculars, not peeping in windows, but watching another neighbor directly across the street from his house cutting down a tree in his yard, the chain saw sending up heavy working music. She had seen many of the lower limbs sawed off with a long-handled, curved saw. One limb had separated with a resounding crack, bringing her to her front room windows.

Her alertness to surroundings brought George Thresher to quick attention as he stood deep within his garage. Without surprise, she realized he never parked his car in the garage, often leaving it curbside overnight, or in the driveway on snowy days. She passed over quick getaway with a quick shrug. "Too much TV," she muttered.

Still, motionless as a watchman hearing suspicious sounds, she wondered for the first time ever what she didn't know about her neighbors, especially Thresher and the man at the tree, Gregory DeFilipo, both men the most recent arrivals on the street, perhaps each less than a year, DeFilipo coming first with a moving van full of furniture; Thresher a week or two later ... with a suitcase on his first visit, and a few items delivered in the following weeks.

With an added assumption, she figured that Thresher never closed the garage door, even in the winter. "Probably broken," she said to herself, "and he's only a tenant," which she knew with certainty. A woman on the street had told her she heard him at the post office asking the clerk about mail delivery and being overly serious about how long the mailman had been delivering the route, which was at least five years.

"I'd best keep my eyes open," she vowed one time as Thresher made another of a series of notes in a small notebook, thick as his thumb, which he would carry in a back pocket of his pants. As a result of this promise to herself and the existence of Thresher's notebook, she dug an old notebook out of a cellar desk that yet carried an open entry, a lone entry in the notebook that read, "The Secrets of my First Love," so "titled" and then hidden away for half a century before use found it for a new cause.

That entry made her look in a mirror, saying aloud but to herself, "I hope none of the ladies ever sees this: she had scratched out the previous entry and simply printed a new title, saying, "Contemplation of a Neighbor." At this point of time there were more than three dozen entries, some at length descriptions of an hour's activity in the garage as Thresher continued his watch, some as cryptic as, "I am dead sure that T. has a cache of weapons and ammunition in his garage; he practices just the handling of a handgun, but never firing it: makes me wonder if he's a secret policeman, a government agent, an assassin, or a plain thief at long planning."

It also brought the echoes back from wherever, her husband of 35 years, Eric Stanvyck, saying, over and over again, "Agnes, I fell in love with you the very first time I saw you at Odell's that Saturday afternoon. I'll never forget how that rushed through me, like I was a receptacle." She knew the minute he said it, each time, that it was a coded expression, a twist of the word receptacle, and loved again his humor and inside jokes, and laughed especially at that realization, like he had never left her, not ever.

An added note, in her blocky printing, said at a quick read: "He deserves all my attention, for I know I am the lone soul at watch in the neighborhood. Even Bitter Sally, two doors down from me, has never placed her eyes on him this way." She was supremely content at that entry, and with the accompanying image of binoculars being brought up to Thresher's eyes at the deep end of the empty garage, jostling her curiosity again, for the hundredth or so time.

What began to bother her were the unknown and obviously unseen activities that Thresher had engaged in before she first noticed his suspicious dedication to the neighbor across the street from his garage.

"I'm glad it's not me he's watching," she said to herself on several occasions, and each declaration accompanied by a shrug either of fear, realization, or mere curiosity. Such self-searching made her bring her whole adult life story into focus. There were petty quarrels with a few neighbors, including Bitter Sally, an argument with Bitter Sally's husband that eased her feelings toward Sally, an argument with the neighbor next door about both snow and mowed grass and fallen limbs ending up on her property in unseen hours, which a friendly policeman squared away with a mild threat to the neighbor, and a small dog problem with another resident on the street who, after challenges about clean-up operations ensued after loud discussions on the matter.

Agnes Stanvyck's own neatness, about herself, her property, her whole world, were accepted as OCD offspring of her character. Such a dedication carried itself to her catching careful eye-fulls of George Thresher, and indeed, extended to any and all visitors that came to his home ... which were few and far between, but nevertheless entered into Agnes's notebook. There were times she wished it was three inches thick and full of his life from his first breath ... and last study with his binoculars. She, of a sound mind, refrained from a drastic creativity that might swing through her mind with threatening promise.

"So, I'm the neighborhood's Peeping Mary. Someone has to do the job or they could walk away with half of it, all of it, or one of its kids." She never said who "they" were, but kept that refrain fresh in her mind, and she even ventured to the local Salvation Army's used goods store to buy herself her own binoculars. "Even Steven," she said. "What's good for the gander is good for the goose." After a few turns at familiarity, she had no trouble focusing the binoculars directly on her lone subject.

Then, one morning, Gregory DeFilipo's tree stripped of limbs all the way to the top, the top itself sawed off the day earlier (with some ladder difficulty for DeFilipo caused by a silly argument with his on-looking wife), the sun just coming on for a promising day, the sky a mix of golden blue and small pockets of street dust tussling with a slight East wind, Agnes heard the sound of an automobile and rushed to her window in time to see a black vehicle, the shiny black, boxy, rental type, slip into Thresher's garage and the door close down behind it, quick, official, some secret commission underway for sure.

Agnes desperately wanted to follow the vehicle whenever it left, sure that some part of this mystery would be unveiled, but she'd have to abandon her current spotting station. That'd leave uncovered any new information or activity that might occur.

Of course, she thought, I could get Harry Parrent to cover for me, only two doors away on my side of the street, but I'm sure the laughter would eventually start running up and down the street, and me the subject of the whole mess. That'd be too difficult to face, never mind owning up to it.

Deciding to remain at her station, she sat in her favorite chair, the Thresher house and garage in full view, the sun soon enough casting a shadow of the stripped tree mere inches wider than a needle, and falling across the Thresher garage door as though a pointer was being used by a teacher to direct interest to parts of text on a blackboard. She harrumphed at thoughts of pertinent words, a related message, a secret exposed.

All her mental wanderings kept her in place, in her chair, past the supper hour, when Thresher's garage door flew up and the black car sped off just as dusk began to settle.

The garage door stayed open ... for three days ... and for three days she did not see George Thresher for one second in all that time, which indeed began to worry her: Was he sick? Did something happen to him? Did his visitor, the hastily departed visitor, do something to him?

In a sudden moment of clarity, and anxiety climbing its own walls, she decided to call the police and tell them some of what she had observed.

"We'll check it out, Ma'am," said an unknown policeman, "and we'll let you know. Thank you for being alert." With that response, there came a sound reception for the first time in her neighborhood mystery.

Ten minutes later a police car pulled into Thresher's driveway, knocked at both the front door and the rear door and an inner entrance door in the garage, with no obvious entry. The lone policeman looked in several windows before he hastily called on his phone and then broke down the front door.

Agnes was the first neighbor on the scene, before an ambulance and two other police cars arrived, and officers began stringing a crime scene ribbon, bright yellow, around George Thresher's property. For a very short time the yellow ribbon blowing in a breeze made her think of a merry-go-round

A plainclothes policeman, flashing his badge, crossed the street and introduced himself to Agnes. "My name is George Miles, Detective Sergeant in your police department."

He looked directly into her eyes. "You the one who called this in, Ma'am?" He was husky, round-faced, half a scowl and half a smile on his face, from which she couldn't really distinguish his true state, but she noticed an official sense about him, not stated, perhaps ingrained by experience. It brought a little comfort to her, even as she realized she had not yet seen anything of George Thresher, upright or flat on his back, though she knew there was more revelation on the way.

"Yes, I did. I saw him out every day, around the house." She almost choked on the lie. "When I didn't see him for several days, I thought I'd better call. Has something happened over there, Sergeant?" She pointed her finger at the house across the street.

The detective did not answer her question but put another one to her. "Did you think to call him or knock on his door."

"I've never spoken to him. Never met him really. He was a loner, it seems, and kept himself inside." She was almost choking on another lie. "The thing that bothered me was he never shut down his garage door until the visitor came the other day and parked in his garage and the door was closed right away, the garage door."

"I wish we had the registration number of that car," Sergeant Miles said, "so we'll have to ask the neighbors."

"336 dash 348," Agnes said without a second's hesitation.

The detective wrote the number in a little notebook, with a firm shake of his head and a curious grin on his face. "You're quite sure of that number, Ma'am?" He smiled again, making Agnes believe she had shared her soul.

"Yes, I am." She said it decisively; it was probably all out in the open without her even knowing it. "When the garage door was closed, it just sent me reeling. He never closed that door and parked on the street all the time. Even at night. Ask the other neighbors. I'm sure they all know it, like the man next door who's been weeks trimming that tree of his to take it down someday soon, I'd guess." Nervously she added, "May I make you a cup of tea or coffee?"

The detective coughed up a small laugh twinned with a broad smile, as though he was easing a situation; "By all means, Ma'am, and coffee would be fine."

They were entering her house when the Sergeant Miles said, "You're quite observant, Ma'am. I really admire that in a citizen who keeps his or her eyes open for the good of the community," and finished that observation off with, "Anything else on your mind?"

His gaze went back over his shoulder and through her front window to the house marked off by yellow tape, the tape still blowing in the breeze, as Agnes noticed more of "his people" in the garage obviously looking for fingerprints. Quickly through her mind went an image of her finding a pair of cast-off rubber gloves a mile down the road, on the wooded outskirts of town, and her left hand picking them up by two fingertips ... lightly, the way she threads a needle.

That thought and image by association was rudely interrupted when she saw him looking down at the coffee table where sat her drab-colored binoculars, purest evidence of a neighborhood busybody, handy for ready-use, and his expression not one of surprise, as though he was nodding to himself about a self-agreed prior observation.

It was time, she thought, almost aloud, and Eric would tell me it was so, to own up to all of this. Oh, if only he was here now, I know he'd be enjoying it as much as me.

The coffee was served and Agnes said without any discomfort, "I hope I have helped you, Sergeant. I've begun to put things together myself, using my imagination and my binoculars to suspect that Mr. Thresher was more than he appeared to be, likely one of those criminals who got guaranteed safe living, 'in protective custody' as they call it." She was sure of herself. Every TV show or movie with that thread in it, came with the same twist, fated or otherwise. "Am I right on this account, this episode?" She felt her whole person relax into a comfort zone, her belonging with some righteous force, police, authority, responsibility, personal observation. It made her whole life seem worthwhile. Eric will love this, she mouthed under her breath, busybody indeed.

Locked into her own dramatics, knowing Eric's face and voice resonance and durability coming her way with a sense of gratitude, even a sense of most proper dignity and thanks in some misty kind of notification or award, she began to prepare herself for a special kind of recognition. The focus had shifted from a criminal under protective custody to an alert citizen who has control over her own minute destiny and that of her whole community. For the first time since Eric had left her, she felt complete again.

Sergeant Miles drank his coffee in small sips, nodding perhaps at a nice flavor or a new flavor, smiling at some inner thought that Agnes was sure she'd never know, when his phone rang, and his attention moved from coffee to an unknown voice she could not hear. The sergeant nodded at shared intelligence or interpretation, a frown, a scowl, a half-smile of surprise coming and leaving his countenance. He seemed transferred into a dead-serious state, all of it, the deepest part of it, showing on his face in forethoughts, measurements, and possibilities; revelation would absolutely have to follow.

In a long, often interrupted or interrupting conversation, only her hearing one side of it, with the sergeant finally saying, "You have to be damned sure of that, there is a woman involved, a widow, no one in her life at the present time." Pause and then, "Yes, a widow for a long time, and invested, as you say."

When Sergeant Miles put his phone away, he gravely turned to Agnes Stanvyck and said, "Ma'am, I hope you have a bag ready to pack. You were dead on about Thresher being in protective custody, as he informed on the man who killed him, who is now loose in the city as far as we know, and pictures will be brought here for you to view so that you'll be able to recognize him on sight if he ever shows up."

Perplexed, Agnes said, "What's this about needing a bag ready to pack."

"The killer of Mr. Thresher left a note in the front seat of the recovered sedan saying he's going to get the busybody who squealed on him. He's done it several times that we know of, so you have to move in a hurry. I'll help you and take you someplace they're working on now."

Agnes, nodding, said, curiously, "Did you bring Mr. Thresher here, Sergeant Miles?"

Behind Locked Doors

The last vehicle I was aware of, as I shifted in bed for more comfort, sounded like the old Pontiac I once drove upon college graduation to a first job, this drive shaft noise bouncing off my street, close to alarm. Counting said it was 60 years ago, and that vehicle into a boiling pit of melted steel parts for at least 40 of those years.

It made me sit up, alert, listening for other signals from night's calculator of aging, part of day's end, nightfall, darkness starting from shaded corners day has the least grip on. The whole house, like the whole street, was midnight quiet, loose under the blanket night throws like a host, my mind realizing that this very building was erected in 1742 and likely had strange visitors or guests in its time. I'd not recognize one of them in my own home.

Off to sleep I had gone at last, when an odd sound woke me, like a slippered foot on the floor of the kitchen, 39 feet long, the length of the house, once being two rooms before my tinkering. I did not recognize the motion causing the sound; It was different, like night and day, cold and hot, new and old, welcome and forbidden, all the differences rolled in contorted images.

My hand was on my cane, stashed against the bedpost, sole weapon of defense, the sound was that strange. And a second and then a third slippered foot on the floor, whispers at hiding, at last disguising the hum into an innocuous hum of sorts.

My mind told me where the family was; son in the second-floor back room, above the garage, daughter directly above me, her two sons in the room across the hall from her, all of them good sleepers most of the time. Though my son had adapted a few of my insomniac traits, perhaps hearing the same slight disturbances waking me, but less alarmed by him.

Each of them had said I worried about every little thing in the world, even the things that are not real, that do not exist, are not real in any sense. "Worry wart's the word on you. All our friends know it. The ladies down the street, the guy out back, the old postman who lives up the lane and has known you for 60 years at least. Hell, you're 90 now, so rest a bit more. The world in one piece is not going to crumble all around you."

They'd add, "At least not tonight, not today."

In defense I'd merely say, "I'm only preparing myself for things that might happen. There's no harm in that. It's not wrong to be ready for anything, even death if it wants its way on any of us."

The thought never roamed too far.

But at this new waking sound, with care I sat up on the edge of the bed, to keep the squeaks at their weakest, ready to spring with my weapon.

Somebody was in my house.

When I slipped from bed, a whisper of sound, I swore, five carpeted steps brought me to the doorway to the long kitchen, a dimmed night light across the breadth of the room casting darkness aside, finding instant familiarity with furniture, kitchen accessories and the vague shadows of three youngsters, two girls and a boy from about 8 years old to 15 or so, proceeding as quietly as possible toward me peeking from the edge of the doorway.

One of the two girls, in a whisper, subject to interpretation on my part, said, "Father really promised this to be our new home? There's only an old man close to 100 in our way and his sleepy family that Father has studied. He'll take care of them as soon as they're ready for transport elsewhere. He is the best magician we ever met. I can't imagine how he'll get it done this time. Last time was doomed by the fire that was an accident caused by another old man. We'll have to watch our steps for sure this time. But he did promise us something different this time."

She spoke like an older person, her diction steady, calm, precise in delivery considering the situation, invading a home, knocking someone's world asunder.

My home!

With my cane at the ready, I swung myself into the kitchen as fearsome as I could draw some elements of fear with me, a rough voice, a harsh and loud demand, a sweep of my cane into the kitchen air … and hitting a pan hung on an overhead beam.

The sound ripped through the house and would wake my family.

But an older voice, from the corner, said, "Don't worry, old man, I've taken care of your son in the first minutes of our entry; he is securely bound in his room and will not be able to bother us. The others have been drugged and will sleep for hours until we have completed our takeover of this house, and arrange the proper transfer. We've done this a couple of times and know how to operate a takeover."

Into the kitchen he advanced, slim, ethereal, more a shadow of a man than the substance of a man, carrying an elegance about him, gray in his clothes, in his manner, in his soft and vaporous being, in his grayness absorbing little of light, remaining as he looked at the first instance, something from another world, not the usual housebreaker type I might have seen in a trashy movie my grandchildren watched without judging the content and delivery of the film itself, a piece of junk that merely took their eyes and time, and not their minds, I truly hoped.

I did not believe what I had heard from him, from them, and swung the cane again at the overhead pan, creating a louder sound, the clanging, full of terror and fright, created no stir from the household or the neighbors, who certainly must have heard it, had made calls, sought in some way to determine the cause of disturbance in the middle of the night.

The sound of the smashed pan dribbled into corners of the room as if it had no source of beginning, no swung cane, no loud retort of the cane crusher.

Nothing!

To which there was again no response from my son, no screams about my safety being first concern with him, no challenge to a slim grayness of a man who was accompanied by children on the most intrusive of tasks, home invasion, home takeover.

9-1-1 must have been dialed by someone in the area. The police sirens soon blaring into the night, distant red and blue flashes waking up the whole route of the responding flight of lights and alarms.

Why did I hear none of it, see none of it, hear from my son? These interlopers, this family or interlopers, would rush from here into their coming, whatever and wherever that was, on this good Earth or elsewhere. I was convinced it was unearthly, all of it, every sound, every word, every intuition coming at me.

Was I possessed? Being possessed? Surely the police would come and then these house thieves would get their true punishment.

"Old man," said the father, "nobody is hurt. You will not be hurt. We will lock you in your room from the outside of each door of your room. We have studied your house from afar and know all the spaces and places of it. It will do us for as long as we need it. And we will not harm you or your family."

His voice had become more assured, yet more ethereal, each time he spoke, becoming hypnotic, I thought, as good as he intended it to be. No wave of power, but a mere presence about the place, a kind of quiet takeover, my place now his place.

With calm and politeness, he had the children lock me into my room, and both doors, one to the kitchen and one to a hallway, were closed behind me, and I heard the simple hooks and eyelets being screwed into place, heard the hooks slip into their eyelet moorings: locked up in my own bedroom.

I had no phone. The windows were tight in place. I worried about my unseen son, and those put asleep overhead. I had to settle my fears, find some target to work on, find a way out of this superficial business, this outer spaceness.

I slipped a wire coat hanger from the closet, undid its twists, straightened a good length of it to reach through a door partially ajar, to slip the hook from its eyelet. The doorway to the hall served best, and the coat hanger length passed through the slight passage and the hook came free of the eyelet.

I stood stock still in the silence of the post-midnight slipping about me, opening the door without a sound, without a creak. I was in the hallway with a window. With ease that window opened and this old body, all joints near decrepit, all aflame with pain or foreboding signals of further pain and damage in the aftermath, I slipped out the window, my cane with me, and stood outside, ready to go call 9-1-1, to get the flashing red and blue lights en route to this simple yet abominable takeover of my home fully corrected, the specters put in place, if possible.

But then, in a flash, I pictured the police reception, their disbelief, their fingers wound about their ears signifying an old man at a loss of his mind, a new character of a new crank in the neighborhood: for God's sake, they had enough of them already.

The whole scenario came near solid in my mind, the finger twirling, the head-shaking, the disgust cast into neighborhood ranks, the barber shop, the variety store, the historic house on the next corner, the 90 years of living in one place broadcast like a cheap show on TV.

I thought of my son's aptitude, his mathematical and philosophic mind, his applications with all things electrical and mechanical, from television and computers and toasters to the use and function of every part of an automobile.

I didn't run for a phone. I didn't scream for help. My mind had gone into an upper gear.

A cellar window opened easily. I reached in and hung it wide open with the same type of hook and eyelet used to lock my bedroom doors. With cane hung for retrieval, I slipped feet first, a kind of slow agony in place, but a target in mind, a duty to be done, down into my own cellar in my own home now in the hands of whoever from wherever, these elegant, ethereal gray ones.

If they wanted something different, I'd give them something different.

I found my flashlight placed on the hanger beside the furnace where I had most use for it, flashed it on the full span of electrical units in one corner, and slowly began to unscrew the fuses for each section of the house. The first one was an off-on touch for several passes, and then an off so my son would recognize the activity taking place, then one by one, listening all the while to slightest changes of sound or silence, I shut down each unit in the house so that the entire house went into complete darkness.

The words of curiosity and concern came to me through the floorboards above my head, through passages in walls, which I recognized as those of the invaders.

"It's beyond me," said the gray, ephemeral father of the gray children. "I know nothing of such applications. We best not fool around with it, so it's elsewhere for us, but I'm sure the old man won't mind when one of the others wake him from his deep sleep.

I heard the front door open and close as they departed.

I managed to get two flights upstairs. I hadn't been up the stairs to my son's room in more than two years. He was glad to see me as I unbound the ropes securing him to his bed.

His wink of congratulation said all he wanted to say at the moment, aware of the rescue procedure, fruit of a working mind finding itself at last in the middle of desperation.

The Old Man Who Made Whistles

In a country that had no name because it had no borders lived an old man who lived at the side of the road and made whistles. Making whistles was all he ever wanted to do. Each time he made a whistle and tested it, playing out its tune, he would make a present of it for a boy or girl who passed his small house.

He was famous for his whistles whittled with love.

One day, when he had fallen asleep in a late afternoon nap, the sun warm on his chest where his hands were folded, a man passing by stole the old man's knife that was laying there on the porch. How sad the old man was that his only knife was gone. How sad the children were when no whistles were being made. In town someone said the birds had stopped singing, that the forest was a dark and dismal place that could frighten any soul. Soon the leaves began to fall in the forest. And then the snow fell.

All that long winter the old man tried to remember how it was, the way it was, when he made whistles and why he had no big dreams and no thoughts of grandeur. Happiness, he found, controlled him and his life. His house was a small house and once the forest behind his house had been thick and heavy with trees. Now it was sparser because of all the whistles he had whittled out of its trees. It seemed boys and girls everywhere played his whistles. But the thinning forest still promised nice shade for spring and would again be a fine place to walk. He was convinced of that all winter long.

Like a crocus popping out of the ground, spring came leaping and early. With the light of each new day coming upon the birds, they'd begin to whistle and send out signals to their friends. Each morning the man sat on his rocker on the porch and listened to them. Very closely he listened, picking up every sound that came out of the forest, every peep and every chirp, and every new sound. There was no bird's song that he did not hear. After listening a while he would settle on a sound or a song that best suited him for the day. That's when he used to set off for the forest to find a piece of wood to whittle a new whistle, to capture that sound forever, when he had his trusty knife.

Oh, he'd think, perhaps those days would never come back. He would get sadder by each minute as he remembered how it used to be. In the forest there used to be a kind of magic in his search for the right piece of wood. Without fail that he'd find the right piece. It could be sitting in its place as a nice branch on a maple tree or it could be a strip of oak that lightning had driven away from its home at the top of a tree. Now and then it was the shape of a piece of wood that caught his eye instead of his ear. But it was always the right piece. And he had always given away the whistles that he made, with birds' music in them.

Oh, how he loved songs the birds whistled, and he could tell practically which day of the year it was, or the day of the season, because of the birds that stayed or the ones that already had journeyed far away. Some of the birds would end up way down in the other end of the world and would be gone for months. Some little red birds stayed all year long, singing songs for the old man. He loved the ones who stayed as well as the ones that traveled.

There was still glory in their music but a full sadness sat in his heart while he was without his knife, sadder each day he that could not whittle.

Then one bright morning a new knife was on his porch. It just appeared on the deck. The old man did not know who left it. Some people said it was the mayor who left it in darkness. But that same morning the old man suddenly heard a bird calling from the forest. Out he went and found a piece of wood exactly as he thought it should be. The newly whittled whistle caught the new birdcall perfectly and the old man hung the whistle on his fence.

He was back in business, or so he thought.

But a strange thing had happened: now all the boys and girls knew what had happened, why the old man had been so sad, and none of them took the new whistle away from its place on the fence beside the old man's little house at the side of the road.

Next day the old man heard another special bird, found a special piece of wood and made another whistle. That one too he hung on his fence. But no one took it. The children saw it, but none of them took it. The old man was sad, but making whistles was what he always wanted to do, so he kept at it. The birds kept calling and he kept making whistles and he kept hanging them on his fence. And still, nobody came to take his whistles.

Day after day, for the longest time, he heard the birds and made his whistles and hung them for the boys and girls. Each night he was sad inside his new happiness. But he knew he would never stop making whistles. Birds were beautiful when they sang and his whistles were beautiful when they were played and somehow someone would come along to play lovely tunes on the small shafts of wood.

Soon there were hundreds of whistles hanging on his fence and not a single one had been taken. No boy or girl ever tried to play one or blow air into the mouthpiece or even tried to finger the little air holes. Not a single boy or girl tried one out. Happiness, he thought, might not be the answer after all.

And it was late that following winter the old man became sick and lay in his bed and the mayor and some other people came out from the town when they heard about his trouble. And the old man told them his life had been a good life and he had no regrets except that he wished the boys and girls would come to take his whistles off the fence. But even if they don't, he said, he had been happy making his whistles.

And then, late in the afternoon, the wind began to blow from the edge of the forest. It blew quick and steady down the road and along the length of the old man's fence. The old man and the mayor and the other people suddenly heard the most marvelous sounds they had ever heard, magical notes of every range imaginable, a music to be remembered forever.

And the old man who made whistles all his life closed his eyes as he heard music coming from the strangest organ ever played.

The Lobster Crews Mixed in Murder

The gang from the boatyard, by God you had to love 'em, the lot of them, every man jack of them; braised, poured, scratched, abraded, welded, mucked about by all of life, you had to love 'em. Up front you have to know that those who had gotten nicknames felt honored, for that moniker stuff usually came from within, a private medal of sorts, earned without hoopla, seared forever. Those who hadn't been so acclaimed patiently waited some kind of anointment, slow in coming, taking over like a root, underneath everything seen or known. Some of them had names like Max, Slad, Wilf, Muckles, Shag, RonnieJ, Slip, a feast of designations varied as character. And the sole captain of his own boat in the lot of them was Shanklin Garuf.

To a man, you had to love 'em.

Outside of Shanklin Garuf who had the gift of property, but who stood by his buddies in all kinds of weather, they were interchangeable elements, reliable, quiet, worn in many of their parts by life… to a man. Dip Connors, friend and local detective, said any one of them looking in a mirror might see the form of any other of that crew. Dip said they were, in spite of shadows worn like vague amulets, the most real people in town. Light, he believed, sat in their eyes, a detention, an absorption only distance or knowledge allows. A compression of the ages, a mute exchange of information, like the bonding the Cro-Magnons had no word for.

None of them, outside of a congruent celebratory boisterousness now and then, had ever given the citizenry of Saugus any cause for alarm. They labored much of life, fought a war or two, hurt a foe or two. They tired. They came on age. They were stars and stripes guys without the parade, a kind of phalanx of maturity in dungarees or corduroys, Bruins or Celtics or Patriots windbreakers, ball caps with championship logos from Saugus Little League or Saugus High hockey proudly worn. They ate apple pie with their coffee, drove Chevy or Ford pick-up trucks into or out of the lobster boat landing or the boatyard, and moved as a body into their second millennium.

And then there was murder.

Max Cargo came upon Shanklin Garuf spread-eagled on the dock and right beside his boat. It was just before 5 A.M. A ball of breath grabbed Max where it hurt the most, in the righteous neighborhood, right next door to his heart, a ball peen in a short swing. Old Shanklin was a real pal and Max's breath caught again, the old quad bypass never far away, a scar if there ever was one. The thought leaped through him, Not now! Not two of us and morning still coming on. At length he breathed deeply, clearly.

The sun, still hidden behind Pine Hill in Lynn across the river from the boatyard, seemed to threaten appearance. A sudden fear hit him that Pine Hill had captured the sun, or would detain it. Salt smell rose up from the Saugus River and a breath of April air touched at Max's face with early tenderness, cool alert. Contrast overwhelmed him. One look at the prone man and Max knew he had been knocked asunder and then some.

Kneeling sorely and gingerly, knowing his arm strength was still enormous though his knees had deserted him with cause, the swung peen known still in his chest harsh as a strident echo, he touched the captain. His fingers went electric, a shock of knowledge passing up through them. There was no rise to Shanklin's chest. No apparent breath. No detection at the wrist. The night before the captain had asked for one man's help for the morning and Max had said he'd do it. Max was an early riser but now he had this; Shanklin, and somebody else, had arrived at the dock ahead of Max.

Max called the cops, telling them all he had done was close the captain's eyes, put his ball cap over them. Besides calling them it was the least he could do, being a momentary salutation in its own right. Contrasts still eating him, he felt irritated at the pretty morning as it came down on him, coming with a lazy stretch out of the eastern marsh with flooding sunlight. The early chirping and signature of birds and the shadowing hover of thermal-lifted gulls bothered him, the hushing touch of swells coasting upriver and washing in against the pier supports seemed wasteful energy; morning coming odd without an old pal.

Contiguously, with clarity, with a specter of pictures, he remembered how haunting the loss of Ace Burleson was the night Ace just fell off the dock, how there was only a splash and nothing ever after to fill up Ace's space. Then, with more pictures crying for company, as if summoned from the semi-darkness, came an oblique tenderness he thought might not have come his way before. Calvin Boone rose up, a black comrade in the 31st Regiment in Korea and that association sixty-some years old, that kinship, blistered him with recollection.

Calvin, a dark giant of a man, a unique softness, was just ahead of him on the hill, stiffening, dropping, reaching one hand to touch someone, something. Calvin's hand had found Max's hand. Then that winged obliqueness hit Max frontally and found doors to all parts of his body. Doors opened for the first time in years. To his feet it plummeted like a bird out of the sky, locking him up with the most excruciating tenderness he had ever known. The pictures faded immediately; Calvin went away, Ace went away, Shanklin went away, but the unmitigated tenderness found a lost home and stayed with him a long while. Even later interrogation could not dislodge its wings.

Max knew how the gang would feel, what they would know. After all, they were brothers at the core. From all he had interpreted, this is what he first understood.

Before noon was at hand, Detective Dip Connors talked to the lot of them, counted all of them as mere background to the crime, and began his investigation. Their poker game, near fifty years old and still moving on, had kept eight of the gang on the second floor of the yacht club for most of the previous night. Looking at the roster Dip knew of six knee replacements, three quad bypasses, one hint of melanoma, and two kinda-touching-the-game cases of arthritis. There was not a rock-lifter in the bunch. For something heavy had slammed Captain Shanklin Garuf on the top of his skull, an object such as a rock with a solid, roundhouse, over-the-head kind of swing. Dip had assured himself it was not the swing of a card player, not a poker player.

"You saw nothing. You heard nothing. You remember nothing out of the usual with Cap and any acquaintance. No arguments or ill will. Have I got that all straight?" Dip had them all on the first floor of the yacht club, at the small bar. They stared at him the whole time he was talking, knowing he was at his work no matter where it took him. His eyes were bright, his gaze firm, his mouth moving with a slow deliberate measure. A shine sat on his cheeks and forehead, as if the tie he wore was knotted out of place.

For a dozen years he had been out of the uniform phase and into detective work. They knew he was a plodder. A draft horse. Slow but relentless. "I am going to need help on this. I am counting you all out of this and all in it with me, right up to our necks." The pause was electric. "I know he was one of you. That counts with me. It always has. I know each one of you like I know my own brothers. That counts." Dip knew he could have written a biography of each one, beginning with a deck of cards and discrete copies of DD-214 service separations.

Some of the yard dogs played 45, some Hearts, some Cribbage. The games were important to them, filled their days and nights when at them, and with talk about them when away from the tables. The games were in the back room of the yacht club, on the first floor, a most modest building scratched against the river bank. Most of the money of the yacht club, for it was a meager place to begin with, more a clubhouse than a boathouse, was on the poker table and that had to have its own protection from noise and other surprises, therefore its home was on the second floor, back end. Wilf Gamin was the only non-card player in the lot of the gamey crew. Odd, loose times for him were spent scribbling in a journal. "My mother always told me to keep a record of my life." He had sixty-two notebooks of that life. None of his pals had read a single page. No one pushed him for show.

A few days later Dip was talking to the chief: "Their hard lot is their history, not in any current malevolence. They're not thieves or murderers. They're old laborers, they're card players, they knock down nothing more than a few stiff drinks once in a while. To a man they've paid their dues of one sort or another. Seen a kind of hell that they've put behind them, until this." He pointed at the crime folder on his desk. It said Shanklin Garuth, Boat Captain. It also said Murder in capital letters. "That lot of men all served in one war or another, except Slip who was never able to do anything like that with his bad arm. Had a couple of POWs in the crowd, Europe and Korea, couple of Bronze Stars, a Silver Star too, I bet a half dozen Purple Hearts, but no story tellers. They wear their travels well as they can. The kind of guys I'd want beside me in hell or down an alley come a troubling night."

"You think this was for robbery?" said the chief. "Somebody caught in the act? Somebody hit the captain with a board or a spike or a chunk of iron? No report of anything missing, if there was anything there on the boat in the first place. What about revenge for some old cause? What about relatives in the mix?"

"That'd be pure guess work, coming up on that," Dip said. "Cap plugged along in life before and after an old aunt left him some dough to buy the boat, and that was damn good number of years ago. I think in '76. Don't know any harsh words ever spoken about him. None he said himself. They swear that to a man. Trouble is some of them don't have a hell of a lot of keen memory any more, hazy being what might describe it. And some of them will be gone before this gets closed for good." He filed the folder in a desk drawer, the move and the thought of mortality being punctuation at its best.

"Well, we'll see what comes out of the relative angle, what else touches on the edges."

The chief patted Dip on the back, then said, "I know I've been here a lot less than you, and I can't always agree with you, but someone would think you think the sun rises and sets on a bunch of boatyard turkeys. They are not the end of the world, Dip. They are not hero class in the purest sense. I don't know how all this wraps up in you. You and them." He nodded at wherever in the outside world, but was signifying the boatyard and the quintessential gang without a doubt.

"Come time, chief," Dip said, "and you'll know the difference."

It was a month later, Phil's Nearby Restaurant was dim, Tommy's Plastic Shop shuttered, the boat yard and docks quiet, the yacht club downstairs empty late at night, the crew of them in the back room upstairs. Not at poker but at talk.

Sledge Crafton, noted for his strength and mostly inertia of the mouth, his eyes deeper than normal, said, "Old Dip's been through us and marked us clean, but he's that known bloodhound he swore he'd be. If he keeps getting stumped he'll be back. Appears like he's got nowhere yet and nowhere to go, so he'll go over the whole track." He nodded his head and added, "Time and again. Time and again." To a man it was acceptable bitching.

"Christ, Sledge," advised Slad Glasko, "he knows none of us had a hand in Cap's death. What's he coming back for if we ain't got nothing for him?"

"Way he works, Slad, knocking things together. We saw that when old Henry was robbed and knocked around a year or so ago. He got to those wise-ass kids because he wouldn't let go. So we know he's going to be around. It started here and will probably end here, whatever the route takes him. What we got to do, and why we said we'd come here, is to do the same thing ourselves. Hell, we owe it to Cap to do anything we can, what he's done for us over the years. All I know is I know nothing but I'm here. If it's only to shake something out of the damn trees, I'm for it. We're all for it. Does anybody know more than the nothing I know? Sheet, I feel so damn ignorant it hurts my balls."

Long into the night they talked and never came past their ignorance of the whole situation, and especially the night in particular, all at their games and then all at their sleep. None of them, except Max, ever scratched at daylight without an effort for a good number of years, Max the morning insomniac.

"Cap could get most things from me," said Tyledge Bracknus, "except the goodness from my laying in in the morning. Couldn't a got me out of the sack with dynamite that day, way we played that night." He looked at Slip, remembered the look on his face that night and offered, "You gotta remember that last draw, Slip. I been thinking about luck ever since, way they came up for you the last hand out, was all of 2 A.M. by then. That was shit luck, man, shit luck of the highest order. You must be paying for it yet outta the winnings."

Slip nodded his agreement and said, "Lady Luck with the cards always takes a turn where you might never expect her, so you don't brag on her or ask her to dance with you more than you ought. More often than not it's Ladies' Choice." For the sprinkling of smiles he nodded in self-agreement, an adage coined in the boatyard.

They talked for hours. Nothing clear, open, or previously undisclosed came out of their communal efforts. Dawn was threatening. They split and went to their sleep. Some of them into dreams as quick as a snore. Some rumbled thinking about Cap being slipped in from behind by an unknown person, the hand swinging hard, the crunch on the head. Nothing came from memory or dream.

And so it was with Dip Connors, two additional months parked on top of the case, as if it is to be buried as deep as Captain Shanklin Garuth. At the station he tells the chief he is buried with nothing all atop him, him and his case. "There's no clue, no recognition, no witness, absolutely nothing to even get hold of. Buried under nothing. It's all so clean, so damn clean. There has got to be the first piece of the puzzle just lying around waiting to get picked up by thumb and forefinger. Snapped up. I know it." His eyes narrow their sudden intensity. "Guess I'll go back again. Them boys be mad as hell seeing me come back so soon, nothing in my hand."

Dip entered the boat yard from the parking lot. He stepped onto the small dock again, the evening sun bouncing off the small swells of the river, the clear smell of the ocean alive on the river. He swore he could hear Shanklin Garuth trying to talk to him.

Muckles Brown, looking out the window onto the river, said, "Dip's back, boys. He's coming in again." They turned as Dip slipped in the side door like a man hunting deer, soft shoed, quiet, not looking to startle anybody.

He was thinking to himself, as he looked at them looking at him: I know each one like I know my brothers. I'd trust each one like I'd trust my brothers. Is there anything I never knew about my brothers? Anything unknown about these guys who I really like? There was nothing unknown. At least of a value in this case. It was only when he looked at Wilfred Gamin that he knew at least one thing was unknown… how Wilf had looked at life in the pages of his journals. What secrets were there? What secrets could be shared? What small tidbit might come alive from his years of observation? He had to try, he vowed. There's nothing else.

Again, as it had before, the thought came that he could write a biography for each one of them. Obviously at the moment Wilf Gamin was the prime object of a ready portrayal, and Dip could remember drawing him easily and carefully out of a car wreck a good dozen years earlier, both ears torn, his jaw broken, part of his scalp pealed back as if a skilled tomahawk had done its work.

Wilf's words came back as clear as the night they were uttered. "Don't blame Briggs, Dip. It wasn't his fault. Some jerk crossed the road right in front of him. He yelled to me to look out. It wasn't his fault." Then Wilf had fainted dead-away and was unconscious for most of two days. Wilf, he also remembered, had come out of high school and went right into the army, Korea on the horizon like a dirty word and some of his pals over there mixing with the Chinese.

The night in front of the church, just before Wilf left for the army, came back to Dip. "It's better me than some of them, Dip." He motioned to some of their pals down the street waiting for the dance to get over and the girls to come out. They were making crazy noises, making gestures at the sky, then in sudden embarrassment cooling abruptly as though people were looking at them. "I'm more ready than they are." The stance was not bluster; it was concrete.

And Wilf was right. All of 20 at the time, Wilf came home with a Bronze Star and a Purple Heart with a cluster pinned on his chest. Never once had Dip ever heard Wilf Gamin talk about his service in the army, about Korea, about firefights, about the Chinese. And it was at that exact instant that Dip Connors realized full well that everything the man knew was most likely entered into his journals. Dip was willing to bet the whole Korean scene was included in the journals, every battle or engagement no matter the size, every comrade at his side, every remnant scar; it would have been the way the man did it. Rather than breathing it, boasting of it, he had applied it with ink.

And if there was anything out of the past concerning Shanklin Garuf, Dip was willing to bet it was there, part of history, entered by hand, in Wilf Gamin's journals, in one or more of the known 62 journals the man had created.

Dip asked Wilf to step aside, into a corner of the yacht club. "I need some talk with you, Wilf. It's damned important to me and to Cap, but I need you agreeing up front with it. Maybe I'm coming at you odd or you might think out of reason, an invasion of privacy, but I'd like to look at your journals. I want to know if there are any leads there I can follow up. Any wild ass connections you've forgotten that might give me a clue, maybe something trivial to you but a sparkler in my eyes."

The first sense of imploration came from his puckered lips. "God, man, I have to start someplace. I'm getting nowhere as it is." He looked back over his shoulder at the gang of them, like a cluster of warm pleasant ashes from an old fire. "No need to share what I know with anybody. Strictly between you and me." Dip's hand fell on Wilf Gamin's shoulder as strong and as sure as a handclasp might have been between the pair.

Wilf nodded. "You're the boss, Dip. I don't play games with that stuff. Don't share it because it's mine, even though all of them are in it." He nodded his head back over his shoulder to the boatyard gang. "That's most of my life right there, Dip. Just about most of it. That takes some kind of appreciation. If you think going through my stuff can help, be my guest, but it's all between you and me. There are a few observations I'd rather not share, if you know what I mean." He nodded over his shoulder again. Dip could feel the robust squeeze of promise, demanding promise, in Wilf Gamin's words. "And then again, there are things in there I can hardly remember writing, never mind the thing happening itself. It's weird but it's like I've been a stranger my whole life."

Wilf turned his face fully to Dip. Deepness came with his voice and that sudden depth filled with both reach and annunciation. "You ever feel you're not quite what you think you are, Dip? Ever get that feeling down in your boots that somebody else is wearing them? I mean, honest to God, do you?"

The most honest facial expression Detective Dip Connors ever saw came to him from the quiet man standing beside him, looking back at a group of fast friends, looking back at his whole life. At once, from some distant point within or without, he was not sure of the point of origin, the small town detective had a sense of unknown proportions smashing through him. And he knew a sudden clarity, that a true observation had come from the mouth of a quiet man he never would figure for such a conviction. Here was an Adam and Eve man, a representative man, the core of his pals locked into his own being; he was one and all. The thought staggered the veteran detective yet he could feel a resolve as hard as a rock.

Three days later, cored to the task, oblivious to all else around him, Dip was digging. His handwriting is so difficult, probably thinks it's coded he does, or wants any reader to think so, but I have fathomed it: Dip Connors muttering under bright light working hard, three days at it beginning to take its toll, being assessed.

He read. He screwed his eyes down to the vast pages. Damn, he muttered, I thought I knew everything; the lights lit up the back of his head, the icons of men at the world, of it. I thought I knew this band of brothers, this cement between men. I thought I knew! Oh my God, I thought I knew!

He was whirling through all their lives, privy to pains and glories, and he knew it, as if he were in on a birth. Fragments of other lives whirling through my mind. The serials of them, the scraps of bark. Elements. Pure and simple, the elements! He paused. There they are, he muttered again, caught forever in the rhythm of the river, subject to the tide, the coming and the going, and I am now part of that rhythm, Wilf and me.

Salvi's mother, in the dead of night, the Calabrese dictate hard on her soul, swinging the razor on her husband's ear. "Sumnabitch, sumnabitch! No more you play the waitress. No more you bring her smell inna my kitchen. Bastid! Now you hear me ever and ever!"

Before him, stripped bare, was Brittan losing a son and his wife in the one accident. The drunk oblivious until early morning in jail of what he had done. Wilf had plied it with his own pain, the words about Brittan, the love the man knew and espoused. They came across the pages to Dip, seven pages damp as dew. He felt the caricature of the drunk, heard the sound of metals impacting souls, and knew at last the lingering pain on

Brittan's face, where a pair of lips held forever an unannounced curse. Dip knew Brittan as he had never known him. And so, he knew Wilf.

Then Bent Crilson leaped his humanity into his eyes; limping through the Death March at Bataan, throwing his life aside with a dash into the jungle, finding escape. It must have been a secret night between the two of them, Dip thought, for I've never heard word one from Bent about his time in the Philippines. Dip could picture the two of them, Bent and Wilf, late, at the back end of the bar, letting out a lifetime of secrets without an audience in attendance, Taps coming out of a Luzon jungle as faint as silent airs. Dip thought he saw a Philippine moon, low, against a tattered cloud, hanging its paleness over them.

It is all staggering, this core of revelation, this endless exposure, and it finds revulsion in the measures of my soul, this personal affront, this breach of sibling parapets. How could Wilf stand to make such a record? How could he bear so much pain and so much glory? What manner of man could contain all this knowledge and never, never once, spill his guts, air out the whole world of being? Oh, what courage, he thinks. What resistance. What boon companionship. What dread.

He is crowded by this knowledge; his breast beats.

"She was pregnant," Muckles said, "and tried to rid herself of it. God, man, I killed her. It was all my fault." A hundred years of memory, it seems, collapsed down on Dip as he read. Sweet but revolutionary Carrie Thurbitt at the turn of the river, her dress snagged on the bank by an old car bumper, a classmate in her last turn at water. Out of the dim past he remembered the ceremony, knew the exact temperature of the chill wind at Riverside Cemetery coming through the trees and up the narrow avenues as Carrie was put down to rest, her aborted child someplace in the other world. Muckles to this day toting that barge-like weight across his back almost fifty years worth.

Dip Connors at a library of lives.

There were reams of revelations; some made him bow his head, some creased him with a smile, and then, on his third late night, deep in the journal begun in January of 1996 he sat straight up in his chair. A small remark, an aside of sorts, that painted the scene of animosity, of threat, around Shanklin Garuth. Dip shuddered to think it might have been said by one of the boatyard gang, and when he turned the page the culprit was named, a Townie but not one of them. A known bad-ass guy that had given Dip fits a number of times. But not one of them! Not one of them!

It was, he knew, a place to start.

All it took, after reading the journals of a quiet man, was for Detective Dip Connors, Saugus stalwart, to start his walk down the front walkway of the troublesome Townie, who broke and ran at the sight of the bulldog detective descending on him.

And Wilf Gamin, ever quiet, never said anything about what he couldn't remember writing, not wanting anybody to know that he had already forgotten some names. That was terror enough.

85

Eulogies for the Ferrin Street Outlaws

*(Header note: Some slight inaccuracies may occur here about
Charlestown, MA of 1935 as I had to depend at times on other people's
memories and hazy postulations of dinner-table stories and off-handed
remarks thrown as parting dictates by well-intentioned folks, yet their
otherwise stable contributions are the basis of facts posted herein, with
the added explanation that those same dictates came to me many years
ago and have, as often as they survive, been touched by age, forgetfulness,
accuracy and possibility.)*

It has come upon me, one, as a survivor of the group that was
formed by a bond in our Charlestown youth, and, two, as one who dwells
daily in mustering words to present to the reading public whose tendencies
favor words of their language to come to them in suitable presentations,
or, as one of them might have said, "in understandable clutches being
enough for me, and at separate attempts," meaning, I suppose that he liked
to read as little as possible but liked what he chose to read ... and that's
being selective from the git-go.

Seven of us were in it from the start, and stayed at six of us when
Joey Riley first knew, with due certainty, that he wanted to be a priest,
that it rode in his mother's heart and mind from the moment he was born
in the third tenement building, left side of Ferrin Street heading to where
the sun sets on good days. Joey first saw light from a third floor window
on "an alley only as wide as a kitchen table top." His father had said that
at the very beginning, wondering how he was going to feed another mouth
at their long, thin kitchen table squeezed against one window, mere hours
of sunshine coming downward on a tough slant on early afternoons.

Such babes, boys, men come "tagged" with eternal promise of one
sort or another, whether it is at the call of the good Lord or the call of the
street, two starts at the head of things in good old Charlestown, beside the
Navy Yard, City Square, the "El" that's bound for everywhere else, and
Ferrin Street where once a part of a cellar held a secret meeting room
which, most likely now, is gone with the ages, rebuilding, re-construction,
new looks of these times.

Joey, once released from his first vows of faithfulness to the other
Outlaws, knew a sudden spurt of joy as realization set its grips on him by
letting him go free of the devil's fear of being caught stealing, theft at
great odds but quick riches, burying his mother before her time, allowing
his father to cough up all the earlier stories of his growth, the sudden and
apparent stuffing of his wallet, his deep pockets, that were seen all over
by many others in that squat neighborhood running from City Square to
Chelsea on the other side of the bridge with the high arch over the Mystic

River, where movement over that arch might often mean escape, new digs, a fresh collection of neighbors whose hands and fingers touched upon labors without question.

The rules binding the Outlaws were simple, direct, came of group discussion without a word of dissent: sworn for life, no signs or symbols or traceability of any kind (meaning no signs or tattoos or single or minor letters on the fingernails, under the armpits, in the crotch, "no idle talk unless we're all here at meeting," no gathering as a group at the Kent School but mixing with other Townies at their lessons, play, recess, routes to and from home, and with our own identities locked herein forever, meaning "be sworn or be cursed." That thought, that covenant of the ages, for the ages, was born within us, so we are blessed and honored by these weights we carry like backpacks being moved away from any starting line.

The Outlaws, in spite of appearances, goals, purposes, came with our own beginning, our own Big Bang. Every penny found, lifted, "scotched off some counter or someone's tabletop, was delivered in later darkness to our mothers' kitchen tables, each one like a shrine of emptiness for the long stretch of some days upon days. "Pennies," as we spoke of them, was a way of including other gifts that shone with coin's brilliance, a bunch of bananas, a loaf of bread from the Bond Bread bakery plant, a can of soup off a store shelf, a single apple or a dozen, a watermelon almost as big as the least of us, but "pennies" to a taste said it best, with an easy finality that our mothers could muster.

Our mothers were appreciative but blind to our methods, to the last of them, for they had in all cases a clutch of kids at their often barren table waiting for the first gift of the day .... stovetop toast, cereal without milk, oatmeal in saucers, cups, small bowls as it was mixed with water heated on a black stovetop.

Billy K. brought that slogan, "be sworn or be cursed," from deeper in his reading than most of us, as he recounted its beginning when it was first used, applied, accepted for life by our small collection of Ferrin Street boys, adolescent, wise for our age, enough seen of elders of the street to form the "illicit corporation" as one elderly neighbor put it from his rocking chair oftentimes placed in sunlight on the brick sidewalk heading east towards the Navy Yard, the road to the Mystic River Bridge, to Chelsea, to points north.

It is supposed that that neighbor, most likely in his very early prime, was enlisted, joined, stood in the ranks of a similar organization, that he too swore an allegiance to the group which may have lasted through some of the earliest tough times long enough for his neighbors to point accusative fingers at them, at him, though he apparently has outlasted most all his appositive finger-pointers. Off a ship in the harbor, met by a cousin, dropped into the Charlestown funnel on his first day in the new land, the new opportunity, the new version of poverty and hunger as the daily grind of life.

The Rileys luckily moved away from Charlestown, and the Kent School, when Joey was 9 years old, so he could get a different start on his priestly endeavors. Some of us, maybe two or three of us, if gathered again, might be able to say we saw him one time when he came back to visit, to bless an aunt who lay on her death bed and who had summoned him for the blessing.

We were standing in the window of The Townies Publican on Bunker Hill Avenue, at attention at 3:30 in the sunlight of a June afternoon, when we spotted our one-time mobster leaving the three-decker where his aunt died that same night, and we had to lift a glass or two to Joey and his aunt in the unsuccessful administration of a prayerful "amen" by and for the pair of aunt and nephew of the Av.

We figured they still belonged to Charlestown, though they had moved away, for good for her, though we never saw Joey again. He ended up in a parish in Pittsfield on the other side of the Berkshires, about as far away as you can get from Charlestown in the whole state.

Ricky "Rags" Johnson was shot by a cop when he broke away from the back door of the City Square Bank, the bag of bills clutched in his hand. Dean "Zack" Weathers fell off a crane and was impaled on an iron fence. Al "Nugs" Boatwright, early into two unions, one being marriage and the other being the Iron Workers Union, Local No. 7, and moved across the bridge to a house on a hill in Chelsea, had seven kids of his own, all boys, all great athletes, all winning scholarships to Boston College, Notre Dame or, the youngest, to Harvard College. and who now is a sports agent for several Patriot teammates. (We don't see him anymore even though we've gone to all the Patriots games at Fenway Park, Harvard Stadium, and their final home at the Gillette Stadium at Foxboro.

Jon "Stash" Podgurski, after a few abortive attempts when he didn't know what the hell he was doing, opened a bar in City Square that became a fast favorite of the locals and was now and then visited by members of the Celtics, the Bruins, the Red Sox and the Patriots, which signifies a kind of chain connection between professional athletes looking for a good time, at a place where a hard-nut boss says what's what in the joint, and keeps the peace and order in line for comrades and big league teammates at leisure.

Peter "Dutch" Barry, who loved numbers and any activity that dwelt in or on or around their manipulations, became an accountant, got into hot water with a couple of clients, left town, and hasn't been seen since, probably changed his name to accompany the many dollars he carried off with him.

Our mothers didn't complain about the small gifts of pennies nickels, dimes, bananas, bread loaves, soup cans, now and then some bag of groceries swiped from a door stoop, a front hall during difficult ascension, from the back seat of an old Ford visiting from the hinterlands where "someone local" might have migrated to Lynnfield, Wakefield, Melrose, those "way out" localities promising a better life at least for the time being.

"Glory be to god," one mother of the lot might say, last night's hunger crossing her table once more, the empty table lingering with its deep voice, its shallow identity. "There's this clutch of bananas on the kitchen table this morning, not a sound reaching my ear during the whole of darkness, and himself still on a late shift at the Navy Yard, or gone for a week or more on one sort of train or another, and out past Pittsfield or Wilbraham or some other country on the other side of the mountains this state wears and wears and wears, and the pitiful few dollars he earns per the day of his labors.

And then, at last there's me, the last of the lot. I was the lucky one, food not begrudged, but fed another way, by another meal, the words rich, full of founding and reason and images so great they burst within me; my grandfather told me all his stories over the years, repeating every one until they burned against my heart, spilled themselves for me, and I caught the tremble from them, the burst of ideas they carried, the hours of joy they delivered, never knowing they kept me in place often for hours, even whole evenings at a time, thus off the streets, away from the others, until they all had paid their dues one way or another, or escaped to the hills, the woods, across rivers, bridges, connections of any kind, including the freedom of choice that littered every path.

As it is, the city has many births of the same body, the same crucial first breath that might be loaded with dust, gunsmoke, disdain for anybody beyond the family circle. So, in his deepest wishes, upon the wings of words, the magic unleashed upon my hungry brain, the sense of collection began with sounds, alliterations, drama, wonder, adventure of others with the same desires that floated in me, the reach of words at the greatest distances coming to my attention, observation, awareness, from others who surely must have gone through the same episodes in life that I had, listeners all of us, as well as story tellers, characters in and of the telling, leaping outward for touch, memory, continuance, the long trail of words in blossom all the time.

One morning my mother found a loaf of bread, Bond Bread, on the kitchen table, all us kids asleep, my father working a train someplace or at the Navy Yard, three days gone this shift or trip, we never truly knew though he always came home muttering up the stairs of the three decker, his mouth full of taste and terror and talk of sleep until doomsday. Neither parent knew what offspring had brought the bread into the house, how it was "earned" in the first place, as my mother would annunciate, or who else might be seeking its return at that very moment so that we were forced to eat it before it was taken back by true owners; the lot marked, the single-board passport from the window of the next-door building, the board or plank drawn back into its coming for the time being, waiting for the next robbery of fresh bread for the mother's table of any of us Outlaws of Ferrin Street, that said route on a plank between two buildings would crush or panic our mothers to a final end, for sure. But between the slices of such a loaf bread a sandwich might be born to be the heartiest meal of many of our days, bologna at its best.

Miss Finn, the first grade teacher also read stories to us, the magic of other minds, the magic of other lands, characters that came on wings of thought to be, thus proven to this day, the real people of this world but just removed from us by a narrow space in our minds, as narrow as the plank of entry between two buildings crammed together as bodies seeking warmth, love, companionship, or "another night where magic tightens its grasp on small minds."

It happened so fast, we were stunned: Billy Hounshell, from over on Medford Street and not one of our regulars but who sat in the same first grade classroom as did me and my sister at the Kent school, fell off one of those "entry planks," plunging down three levels of side-by-side buildings trying to get into Schrafft's Candy Company, his sweet tooth driving him up there in the first place rather than a partial meal for his family. He took all of them, the Hounshells, and all of us, on that quick dive to death and oblivion and "a sure place in Hell if you was to ask me," soon as light came to us and the sad news of his death ... and damnation.

It must have become window-pane apparent to my grandmother, the bookbinder, that we were doomed for such extinction, for such place of doom, because of a sudden, as quick as Billy had fallen, a truck was at our door to move us, lock, stock and barrel clear out of Charlestown to a little town a few miles up the coast, our kind of doomed forever left behind in the empty flat, the cold sidewalk, the littered alley that bound our tenement buildings as thoroughly as a strip of a small dump of waste, small souls, hungry mouths, sad promises to anyone with half a brain ... and there were lots of such folk in the immediate area.

I figured, en route, that I might be writing my last eulogy, my own, the new name "Saugus" tossed at us as if some wild-eyed Injun was waiting on us for the next terror to be won over, slain, done with, or dropped off, as it might prove, from the end of the world.

But the greenness of it was superb, splendid, overpowering, the leaps and bounds for it almost visible from every corner, field, lot, sudden space on our sudden entry, in a single truck loaded with family, furniture, future.

Grease Monkey Joe

Joe Buffalino danced into work every morning of his 45 years on the job, the other two mechanics, the odd-jobs driver, the two clerks and two salesmen in the office, keeping time on him, counting off minutes until he punched the time clock, saying his hands were already occupied with tools. He predated the hiring of every employee, especially in the sales force.

To a man, and all the buyers of second hand or repaired cars over the years, any motor Joe Buffalino worked on was music at work, a hummer on the open road, a subject of conversation at the barber shop, the pool room.

At their lone competition salesmen hungered for a technician like Joe. "You gotta get him here, Harry," one salesman said to the owner's son, "and I'll give him 5 per cent of commissions. I ain't done that in 20 years of selling road-worn buggies. Not once, and you can bet on that. Jiggsy over there says they come back to shake Joe's hand after they take a rig for a ride. He's a magician, Harry. You gotta know that by now."

"Don't say that in front of our boys. They might not appreciate it." He looked around to see if there were any eavesdroppers for the last word from the front office.

"Hell, Harry, these guys knew that before they came to work here. The whole street knows about Joe. A car stutters and stops out on the highway and any time the driver asks a local for help, they hear, "Get Joe Buffalino out here, from Geary Motors, give him a listen and get a lesson on how to fix an engine, Every time, 'less it's crap f'ever." He added a final judgment, "You get your own one-man advertisement without paying him any extra."

It went on like that for all the years after Joe came out of Korea and his stint in the war where he also earned repute as a master of things extraordinaire. One such adventure found him solving the delivery of food and ammunition up a steep mountain under enemy fire. Such tasks were usually performed by Korean laborers who spent long hours on long trails up mountains. This went straight up from Hell of a sort, Death on their backs, strapped down for good in some cases.

Joe took care of the beast; he jacked up the rear end of a six-by truck, took tires off a set of double wheels, used the inner rim for the power source and the outer rim lugged up and rigged on the top hill and ran a cable up and down that beastly mountain. Those deliveries were clean, quick and body-saving, the Korean laborers getting well-earned rests on that dog of a mountain.

The elder Stetson saying once to his son Harry, "Don't let Joe out of your sight, Harry. He'll carry you off to the moon if he's of a mind, him and Neil Armstrong'd be the pair of pairs."

And some of them knew the humor in Joe Buffalino's blood, a heavyweight's dose of it lurking in the alleys of his mind, along with solutions to problems not yet inserting themselves into daily duties, like switching tools in his tool rack to confuse the silent borrowers of tools, making them face up to their heist of sorts, an embarrassment for the moment, a lesson learned but it did the trick.

The plum of plums would be saved for special occasions, a special customer, a special personality coming out of left fields of customers; the hard liners, the raised voices, the kind that said, "I-know-for-damned-sure-what-ails-this-rig-of-mine-and-you-can't-tell-me-by-listening-and-nodding-your-head-that-you-know-more-than-me-what-ails-it," all said in a singular breath as if it was an ABC of retorts.

Such a customer came on a rain-promised Friday afternoon as clouds loomed in place, not a breath of wind to move them, weekend at hand for the crew at Geary's shop.

Joe was putting the last touches on a Buick convertible with a hood almost as long as a first down 3rd and 4 near the goal line, when his shop boss, Jiggsy Cutler, said, "It's past quitting time, Joe. You got that baby near ready to go? You got big plans for the weekend?" He spoke lightly to Joe, tempered, patient, knowing the value of the man he respected with a sense of wonder to boot.

When the phone rang, Cutler, with a disgusting face, answered, "Jiggsy here. We're about to close down. If you have a problem, it'll have to wait for Monday." He pulled the phone away from his ear, held it aloft, and he and Joe Buffalino heard a panicked voice say, "This is Homer Vastling. I was about to pull three wagons of hay into my barn, and the motor on my rig coughed, kicked itself and shut down. I can't get a peep out of it, the rain is sure to come, and I need the rig fixed."

"I'm afraid I can't help you, Homer. My last mechanic is working past his quit time, and then he's gone for the weekend. You'll have to wait for Monday." Vastling was an eminent farmer in the valley, his holdings spacious, wide, impressive.

"I can't wait. I'll lose three whole loads."

"Cover them with canvas. Buy it if you have to." Cutler made a face in a silent addition.

"I'd have to go to Ellsville to get it. I don't have time. I'll pay double for Joe Buffalino if he's the mechanic still there. Can I speak to him. I'm up the creek on this. I don't know beans about engines or motors besides hoes and rakes and plows. I need help. If it doesn't go on when I turn the key, I'm a gone goose. I really am."

"Well, Mr. Vastling, that'd be up to Joe," as his stance and response had obviously changed, "Joe's weekend, I'd assume, is lined up from the minute he leaves the shop, which is soon." He saw Joe snap the key in the ignition slot and the engine roared into life.

The purring sound filled the Geary shop as Cutler handed the phone to Joe Buffalino, a smile on his face that Cutler wasn't sure was a reaction to the sound of the engine or a genuine contemplation at play in his mind.

"What've you got, Mr. Vastling?" Joe said.

The reply was, "You gotta help me, Joe. I'm in a real bind." The voice was distracted, impulsive, impatient.

"What've you got, Mr. Vastling?" Joe said.

The second reply was almost word for word from the first one: "You just have to help me, Joe. I'm in a bind. I need help."

"What've you got. Mr. Vastling?" Joe said for the third time, and one could almost hear the gulp at the other end of the phone, the reply toned down from a demanding whine to a careful explanation of strife, "It's the engine on my Do–All Buddy hooked up to three loads of hay that have to go under cover in my barn. I called my son over in Reality and he must be busy. He has my tractor, so I'm stuck, Joe, stuck in the muck, or what'll be muck if you can't help me."

Joe knew the answer before he asked, "Is it a Kohler motor on your unit?" He knew them like the back of his hand, outstretched for perusal, stubby fingers at first look, sensitive at touch of steel and its counterparts.

"Yes, it is."

"Okay, Mr. Vastling, I'll have to let my wife know I won't be home on time and you have to agree to do a few things before we get started."

"Yes, anything."

"Take that motor off the Do–All and bring it down here to the shop."

"Yes, sir."

"And you'll have to wash each piece I take out of it, wash and clean and dry and oil up for me. Each and every piece. Understood? I'll need your help to get this done, if you want to save your hay, save it from this rainy day coming down the line to us."

"I understand completely. I'm on it." The phone clicked.

Out-of-breath Homer Vastling brought the small motor unit to the shop, along with repeated and profuse thanks before Joe Buffalino even started his repair work. But tools of the trade were lined up on his bench and he began taking the unit apart, piece by piece, placing each one, one by one, in a small canvas sack for proper care and handling by Homer Vastling, bound now to assist the mechanic. He started the messy clean-up.

Parts practically flew into Joe's hands as he disassembled the engine, each piece extracted went into the collective bag for care by the farmer, the work proceeding at a fast rate, and amazement expressed first on the customer's face and then voiced as he said, "How will you know where to put them back?"

"I'll know," Joe said.

"But how? I don't see any diagram of the motor. How will you know? This is important to me." There was more than plea in his voice.

"Me, too."

"But how?" said again as amazement crossed his face with each word, each shaking of his head, quandary holding him fast.

"With help from you and not questions."

At that point, Joe Buffalino grabbed a handful of nuts and bolts from a container on the bench top and placed them in the bag, Vastling not noticing the transaction. Only Cutler, behind the glass partition at his office, spotted that sly transaction, and a healthy smile crossed his face.

When Vastling had cleaned and dried each part and oiled them, the second bag was filled with all the cleaned parts, and Joe Buffalino started assembling the motor. It took less time than the disassembly, and Vastling shook his head in amazement as each piece was placed into the motor structure.

With one swing of his hand, and a concurrent switch of the motor's on button, the unit began to hum, the music of that repaired unit filling the shop as if a maestro controlled the very air.

Vastling was still in a state of shock, his mind slowly absorbing what he had seen no other man do in his life. The wonder of it all continued to leap around his face, disbelief trying to set itself in place and failing by each purr of the engine.

Joe Buffalino was wiping his hands dry of oil, Jiggsy Cutler was still looking through the glass partition, his own evening still delayed, when Homer Vastling looked down into the second bag and saw a few unused parts scattered in the bottom of the canvas bag, like children lost at play, no way to get home, all alone and nowhere to go.

"What about these?" he screamed so that even Cutler heard him. "What about these? Where do they go?" His hands were on his hips, the stance accompanying his words, a stature in place, a demand, an amazement, an innocent belief yet wicked assumption of catching a master at fault in his chosen trade. "What about these? Did you miss them? What if the motor dies if I get the wagons hitched? What do I do with them?"

Question and curiosity, as well as demand, scoured for enlightenment.

Joe Buffalino cupped one hand at one ear and tipped his head for listening, only the purr of the motor came to each listener, the scattered actors in this small drama.

The soft entrance of Jiggsy Cutler's laughter, from off-stage, came first, seeping into the wide spaces of the shop, toting the unsaid message. It alerted Homer Vastling who suddenly recovered himself, who suddenly placed hands on hips in silent approval of his own first ignorance and realization of what he had just seen, endured, finally embraced, as Joe Buffalino began putting his tools back into their allotted spaces on his rack, his day on the job finally done.

Mom, the Glenwood, and the War Years

My big brother Jim was in the Pacific, I was the lone boy at home with five sisters and undaunted I tried mightily to make a difference, to count the little things needed doing, to contribute as "the big boy at home." Nights I slipped out of bed, sometimes from under an old overcoat worn down by years but made serviceable as a thick winter blanket, to drag that old coat to cover one of the girls shaking the most, shivers in action or note whose blanket was thinnest, the one we took turns on.

Then, chilled to the bone, the cold wind often rattling its terror against the windows of the old house, wearing an old sweater or sweat shirt somehow inherited, I'd slip in beside my mother or father, hang on the edge of the bed but under cover and know the warmth for an hour or so and then slip down stairs to poke up the kitchen stove and feed it with chunky shiny black anthracite from 25 lb bags bought at the local Economy Store. Those scenes were my early teen hours, darkness abounding, five A.M. rarely yet at hand.

I'd become an early riser, a habit that lingers yet into my 89th year; my grandfather having said one time and one time only, "Plant your feet on the floor and go get done what needs getting done before day takes you away." He'd known hunger when younger than me, "day calling on him."

As for the coal furnace in the house, it was broken ten ways to Sunday, had most of its parts sold to the junk collector for pittance or donated to piles for the war effort. Its main frame was cracked and replacement funds not yet available. Two ten section radiators had split in several places and, unable to lug or carry them out of the house, I had separated their sections and carried each section off to war, a tank for the Pacific, a long gun barrel bound for Europe. Such images also included the steel prow on his ship not long after the attack at Pearl Harbor.

Mind you, we weren't completely broke, but food for the gang was our number one need. My father, a former Marine was a guard at the GE, and my mother was a cleaning lady at the same plant; even two paychecks didn't do the full run for seven of us.

But that old Glenwood stove top, where morning toast was prepared for the first comer before my mother would commandeer the whole top of the stove to make breakfast of one sort or another; oatmeal was universal (then and now without surprise), available eggs beaten with additives to spread the yellow yolks for all of us, pancakes under Karo corn syrup in distinctive cans, as common as evaporated milk and as distinctive in memories marshaled by the Depression Years.

Now and then, after a weekend hambone's survival, but hardly intact, there'd be ham and eggs in a variety of preparations and shares, a collection of toasted cheese and ham sandwiches directly from the top of the Glenwood, a round-robin sharing for those standing in line with plates in hand for the most generous offering of morning, a taste that lingers still in this mind along with the faces and chatter that we lived on and for and with, and where each day we moved closer to our own destinies, our own new families, the spread of those memories carried to all points of the compass, that old house there yet in place, the Glenwood in the melt of ages, my lonely tears hiding all these images.

From One War to Another without Choice

I'd lost a brother and remember the headlines, newsreels, songs of bond-selling, gas-griping, and movies too true to hate, the settings of World War II. Those days found the whole Earth bent inwards, imploding bombs, bullets, blood, shrieking terrible bird cries in my ears only deepest sleep could lose if it ventured close.

Near sleep I remembered the nifty bellbottom blues he wore in pictures my mother cleaned and cleaned and cleaned on the altar of her bureau as if he were the Christ or the Buddha, because he was out there in the sun and the sand and the rain of shells and sounds I came to know years later moving up from Pusan, the new war my war.

I never really knew about him until he came home, jumped off a train in Saugus Center (where trains no longer tread) and I saw his sea bag locked on his shoulder. It was decorated with his wife Elise's ink-sketch drawing capturing much of her beauty, and the ultimate map with the names Saipan, Iwo Jima, Kwajalein, the war.

I came awake suddenly, a new internal motor finding gear, revving up.

So I am commanded that this conversation be set with old red wine that brings me out of surging daylight to fill the doorway like a mailman with a bad letter or telegram, the old neighborhoods of the time struck wide with loss. Specters leaped out of that old mixture, the blood of grape, the fine chalk it paints teeth with, a whole day of sunlight collared in a tumbler, a red sunset too far away to tell where it's going. Death at notice.

He went off to that sunset once, around the corner of the barn tipping toward its knees and Sam Parker's garden paving the ripe earth all the way to the Lovett house sitting white as a pepper-mint down the lane, the family about on the land, doorways framed with faces refusing to age in front of me.

When he waved at me he did it with both hands and only later, when it had gone down the mortal chute, was significance found as I remembered the leaning barn's shade swallow him whole, taking one bite of the car. And he was gone with a two-handed wave like signaling Saturday's lone touchdown.

So I have an old wine or two, a buzzed-vine beauty of taste sometimes more like apple cores or flesh from a peach nearer the pit, and hum the old sad songs, scribble crazy designs and whorls on a blank paper waiting a poem up to its knees in mud in my mind, and think about his waving at sunset because I never see it the same way twice.

Often it is pieces I see; his eyebrows thick and dark and sure as cordage; or gray-green eyes wide as dial faces on test equipment measuring tasks I was at and how he appraised with a nod so slight I shivered before recognition; the little off-center tilt of his head in question the way a dog takes a first look at the new neighbor's cat or fingers snapped behind the back; perhaps, deep in the sunset of the second glass, down past the red and purple and fiery collars, past all the striae a shining breaks out in wine, a shadow of him walking across Pacific waters, sea bag shouldered, stride long and unhurried, smiling, waving to us, coming home, gigantic fires fading behind him, awful nightmare blasts, bombs, aerial explosions, fractures of ships, swimming alone, fading too.

I find him in the glass, tall, lean, crowbar true, warm as rubbed pine, immovable as bottom rock, close, reaching, bending, lifting up, still building all our dreams he drafted in darkness in the bedroom the night before the end began.

Telling tales is a sweater too long hung on an iron spike near leather goods of an old horse. One glove, fractured at wrist and thumb, three gardens old, capped on a spade handle, carries its own clues. In the mix is a scythe handle, spine scattered to every degree, two blades dead, holding a hundred years of sweat waiting raccoon's discovery of the slow night of a full moon and wheat fields curling wet. Size eleven khaki waders, hung to dry ten years ago, exhibit river remembrance in deep-scarred veins the way lake bottoms dry, and whisper of accident remnants.

A red and black lumber jacket, buoyant exclamation mark beside the cellar door, rigid as winter pond and still soft behind my eyes, holds the last day my brother knew at my side.

If I were to gather all these artifacts, the yield would be tender.

An infantry of stars swarms the slow sky wide as a Vicksburg field between artillery shots, off-shore cannons of another war tossing an island to pieces. Elsewhere, hard to measure distance, scattered guidon ripples the slow torment of deep passage just beyond Polaris. Near giant Orion's eastward shoulder, a torchbearer pops an impetuous gleam. Small encampments, sometimes sevenfold, tighten their ranks in bright bivouacs, at rest from the sounds of war, the threats of incoming sounds shattering silence among those born for battle.

Others, loners and post guards, circle wide circles like the dog star Procyon at hunting. This vast array does not appall me, though I diminish before its deployment. I have been told, in good faith, that many of these stars are dead, but we know their shining, like old soldiers, long-gone, cement themselves into statues, dim ribbons and old medals whose scriptures fade at sun and slowly, gram by gram, inch toward minerals and memory. beneath my feet this veteran earth slips into the far side of another's telescope.

In turn I remember Lake Hwachon. There was nothing to do on this side, that's for sure. We boated over. There was nothing to do on the other side either, but die, or stand in line, or check out our gear. No rentals. No two-piece bathing suits catching up the sun. No hot dogs in short buns. No sand-oil grit spread. Dale Morgan, a subsequent short-timer, lost a calf muscle to a Bouncing Betty. Oh, there were lots of them, locally-flavored, territorial. They made stupid noises that said, "It's too late, pal." Those were the only kind of umbrellas at this lake, you can bet.

Tony Morocco was luckier at calves, losing both, and everything you can name in between. Waterville west of the Mississippi, perhaps Iowa, used to be his hometown. He didn't like lakes, including this one.

When we crossed on pontoons and rafts and dories with outboard motors, I watched him undo his booted laces, unstring his weapon, set his small pack under his butt. He smiled at me, telling me about water, rivers he must have grown up worrying about. How to hold your breath. We already knew about mortars' wet impacts. Water does them up funny.

I talked to old Ski in Chicago just the other night. He's buried his Japanese wife in Arlington. His daughter is dying. He's sad. He's had so much junk then, and now, it piles up again. He didn't like lakes, not that one, or the one that's sifting its swim of cancer around Chi-Town. Breda, living near Mattoon, says the Old Polack's just not the same, got this old-time look in his eyes, like when we beached and he asked what date it was and counted there, right in the open, his damned points earned for rotation homeward.

He's been a history lesson on his own. He'd been through Frozen Chosen, Hungnam, and all the stops between. Oh, he had a before and an after: the Philippines, Kwajalein, Saipan, not necessarily in that First Cavalry order, and then Chi-ROTC for short years, and death still hanging around him like a turd on the bottom of his boot. And tears on the phone he can't hide, tough old bastard he is, two-wars dying at that.

He didn't like the lake shore either. I bet he still doesn't. I can see him, even all these years later, stepping ashore, rifle down-range, ears picked up, more a cougar than a deer, intent, a Polack with a piece of Apache in him trying to find its way out of his eyes. Maybe a New World Comanche in tow. Perhaps, I often thought, he carries an old Prussian bloodline left over from ancient guard duty.

But lakes have a way of undermining you, make you sit too easy on the fat duff, make dreams and nightmares quick-wedded, stick it to you where and when you least expect it, make it happen. Ski happened. He exploded! I shut that mastery of his out of mind. The known quantities and qualities fail too often, in measurement, in contrast.

But still he's sad and hates lakeside, shore, waters of the giving and taking lake, time. Old General Mac was right; Ski's just floating away on the invisible waters, drifting off, leaving me, finally, way down the line here, like the others had promised, numbers mounting, this strange way of saying goodbye, comrades I met in a hole, the 76-er mm weapons in alien hands, screaming over our heads all that ungodly night, well over half century ago still here.

It stretches all the way home:

Eddie Smiledge was the houseman at The Rathole, racked the balls, collected coin, was a judge with a hundred dollar bill in the side pocket. He smoked cigars thick as cue sticks, ate Baby Ruths until his teeth stuck, sent us home abruptly when our eyes became hazy or midnight slipped like a footpad over the green felt on table No. 4. He did not lend us money, but let the clock work in our favor; at a nickel a game he didn't see the eight ball eight times in the side pocket, and forgot to lock away all the nickel bags of potato chips.

One night we played One-Ball-in-the-Side-Pocket past closing and Eddie sat in a corner waving off the game costs. We walked off under a September moon all the way to Korea.

The night I came back, chevrons up and down, deep new wrinkles struck across my face, measureless but valid, reaching for my yesteryear, a skinny bald-headed man was racking the balls. He didn't know my name, who was home from Korea, who wasn't, who wasn't going to make it, why Eddie Smiledge had drifted off someplace the day after we left ... never to be seen again.

Strangers to Love

I won't coerce you. You can believe what you want about things that happened back in 1944, in that other century, but Willie Kriegslin, of course, never existed, never made love more than a dozen times in a secret cave in Maine with a 17-year old farmer's daughter whose name was Emsie Felton, never escaped from the POW camp near Houlton, never served with minor distinction in the 90th Light Afrika Division of the German Afrika Corps in the Sahara Desert during World War II, never contemplated murder or marriage. You can believe all that... if you want. But I wouldn't. Take it from me.

All that said, love was afoot.

In the dead of silence it happened, at the hour before the false dawn, the sky still bristling with stars, a low moon heating memories, when a voice from outside echoed through the cave. For the third time of this late night encounter, Emsie had borne Willie's weight, fearful each coupling might be the last, her grasp telling him so– and the deep rhythm coursing down through flesh and bone, running with her blood. It made way in her fingertips, in the newly-remarkable span of her thighs, in that place where her heart might have been, now knocked asunder and beating fitfully. Movies had done this to her, and stage plays, and everyday drama crawling through or exploding on those otherwise common days, all exposed to her by her mother who could have been imprisoned by the farm and its insistent, laborious demands. But wasn't. Nor would her daughter be so shackled.

And the young German prisoner helped with his part.

With Willie there were moments, such as at this interruption, when Emsie thought not a breath was left in her lungs, the way wind left her, with a rushing noise and added expectation, like parts of an orchestra coming and going, the brass horns ringing, the violins lingering. Willie had accomplished that from the first encounter. And all of it now erupting simultaneously behind her eyeballs, seeing things that did not exist, not as yet, images of the future carved by her mind and frozen in place... just when the harsh voice rocked through the cave on the far edge of the Felton farm. The voice was raucous and metallic and she immediately recalled a King Lear play in Boston and a stagehand, a musical stagehand she supposed, for battle and storm presentation beating a large sheet metal plate, hanging from the rafters, with a huge rubber mallet. In row three, at her mother's treat, she had shivered away any disbelief of the spectacle.

This night of the cave was in late August of 1944. The invasion of Europe had begun two months earlier, with measurable noise and thrust, on the coast of France, the German campaign in Africa having been shut down fifteen months earlier, and the world going topsy-turvy once again.

Most of the potato crop had been picked and packed off and cellar barrels in many parts of Maine stacked with taters and salted cod. A minor chill slipped in from the northwest sly as an infiltrator, winter's hello fully presumed, its signs known quietly. The days, one at a time, came differently, making announcements on their own selection, nature assisting, demands being made. A few of them were subtle for starters, as high-based color turned with a slow, tempered ignition. Early daylight sky behind familiar silhouettes became, by degrees, a hard blue, stark and clean-edged, as if cut deeply into cerulean ice. And pinnacled. Singular pine trees, at a glance, stretched the Earth for all it was worth, lifting selves mightily. Mountains appeared proud as a woman's morning breasts matching her hipline, blankets astray on the far side of sleep, night tossed aside, messages rampant and understood.

Only Emsie and her brother, now in California, had known about the cave on the edge of the family farm. Nobody else had ever visited there, she was sure. But Willie had found it, all as if she had been waiting for such discovery, and such a man with such a way.

The cave, hidden by the tangle of old trees, was on the side of a hilly ledge, and tipped slightly downward toward the entrance providing quick release for rain or ground water. This made the cave habitable though small; and good for drying out, for secrets, for love making its way at the edge of Willie's escape. Granite reaches seemed spawned from the cave itself, great slabs this end of the earth openly wore as signatures of another era. The cave, calved by a glacier instead of by fire in an earlier millennium, had been formed out of huge slabs, but was no longer a significantly cool place. Graffiti, a long way off, had not touched it yet… though minor fires later on it had, sheets of smoke leaving a texture of smudges, burnt spots, darkened fingerprints. In other caves a world away, Pre-Adamites or Paleolithic people, perhaps, had lingered, drawn wall relics, and passed on, leaving their best interests.

Willie had managed a visit to a cave discovered in 1940 in Lascaux, southwest France, before his assignment to the German Afrika Corps in the Sahara. He was an amateur spelunker and Emsie believed he was born for this cave, though few people knew about it, probably including those Pre-Adamites or Paleolithic peoples. Pure fate was on her side.

But now, before the dawn flash, someone else did know: Elwood Felton, the owner of the threatening, baritone voice.

"Whomsoever's in that damned hole better get their ass out of there right now else I'll fill it with enough buckshot to make 'em a decent burial." His voice was louder than any Panzer sergeant's and Willie Kriegslin stiffened in place.

Felton's daughter, Emsie, 17, not quite bordering on lovely, dreamy but spontaneous, thrill still random in her, quickly draped her hand over

Willie's mouth. "Don't say anything, Willie. That's my father. I'll go. If he beats me, don't hurt him, promise me that. Don't try to kill like you did in the desert. I remember what you said about Gazala and Tobruk and El Alamein. How you were captured. I know you're glad it's over. We're both out of the war now. Promise not to hurt him. He doesn't know any better."

At those words Willie's right hand was cupping Emsie's breast, her elegance and forgiveness encapsulating him. His English was imperfect, but she could understand him, piece it together with apparent ease, smile continuously, touch back. He said, "No officer ever told me I'd meet a girl like you. I am filled. I do not want not to release the riches in my hand. But that voice out there is more than a threat. It tells me I might never touch you again. God forbid that, no, not ever again." Such thoughts rushed him quicker than any image of the prison camp and what was promised him anew because of this aborted escape. "Never have I known this kind of sweetness. The softness you bear. What magic passes into me from a mere girl with arctic blue eyes and dimpled cheeks and artistic hands. Whose flanks swallow me truly."

She shivered again and deepness resounded in him for the first time in his life, a bell ringing for all it was worth, pushing at his skin as if it were to break through and shatter him. "Oh, Emsie, pieces of my soul are being cut to pieces. If I were to die, I swear I'd never let go." But Emsie, even at hearing her father's voice and ever at control, guided his hands in a last pass at mystery, to that near elsewhere where other matters had already concluded.

"Whatever happens, Willie, don't you forget me. Don't you dare. Not ever."

They had enjoyed two weeks of being lovers, two weeks of tempest and tribulation, two weeks of discovery, the old and the new. She had been told everything. Willie had escaped from the POW camp when he followed, at a discreet distance, a Kommando officer who had fooled the Americans into thinking he was only a dumb foot soldier. All through his young war, Willie had been led by such men. For the early years in the army the future was always with the man leading him in battle. Supposedly, that future had changed.

When Emsie's father yelled at the mouth of the cave, darkness had molded everything but Willie's hand. There, that elegance of the lingering breast kept shivering back at him, the messages lasting until that precise moment. A ball of breath, in his chest, held its place, the hunger frozen in form, swearing to last forever. He kissed her one last time and saw the whole movie developing right in front of his eyes. It was all black and white and ran quickly, in a newsreel fashion, with scenes leaping place to place.

Emsie, in her own rush at recapture, saw again the flash of her own recent history, her angled views of Willie Kriegslin from the first moment he had dropped off the tail end of the army truck weeks earlier in her father's yard. She felt all the righteous signals the moment her eyes drew level to this young prisoner brought to the farm on the large truck, along with other German prisoners, to bring in the potato crop. All the commanding parts of her body had been screaming for something like this for months on end. The other parts did not count. Reality, at length, stood on its hind legs, breathed, moved as graciously as a dancer, understood what was about him.

This handsome blond with the wide shoulders began to play the rhythms in her bloodstream. Announcements leaped out of her. She saw where they landed, down in the fishing hole depths of his eyes where something frolicked, counted hours, played back a chorus of answers no other soul in the universe was privy to. Knowledge leaped upon her, found its way home to belief.

The prisoners had climbed down from the tail end of the six-by truck, mostly looking like roustabouts from fairs or carnivals. And there stood blond and wide-shouldered Willie Kriegslin, young POW, starkly blue-eyed and yet somehow innocent in what mild measurement she could muster, it being enough for her. The only place of comfort for her in this whole terrible world, now hurling pieces of hot metal at each other from one end of the planet to the next, was contemplating a handsome German war prisoner, looking lost in the depths of Maine. A handsome boy, indeed, extracted from the hell of his war.

Her heart leaped, a bit in sympathy, a bit in lust, a bit of curiosity riding her for the next few days.

The wide shoulders had come first to her, the near unreal span of them compared to what was left of the young male population in town… all the others called to war… and his eyes so much like the eyes she had last seen on her Golden Lab with his collar hooked on a tree being driven in the rush of the Allagash River's white waters, a look she would never forget. As Emsie might have said to anybody who'd listen to her, she was ready for Willie who, obvious to her, was appointed at this time to come into her life, safely and wholly extracted from the war.

And Elwood Felton, scene stealer, yelled again; "I ain't gonna say it again, mister. Git'n your ass outta there is the best part of advice you can expect, 'cause there ain't gonna be no more." Buckshot came from the shotgun burst off a rock outside the cave, and the noisy blast bounced into the cave, ricocheting off granite surfaces worn smooth by a hundred millenniums. "I knowed you was in there last night. I just waited up for day comin'."

Emsie whispered in Willie's ear, "We're not done yet, Willie. I'll see that true." She moved against his hand, and then guided it in a last touch. "You remember me, Willie, no matter how long it takes. You remember me."

Rolling away from her lover, she sat up and yelled out. "Don't shoot any more, Pa. I'm coming out. Willie and I are friends." She could have sung those words, but her father would certainly be tone deaf to their meaning.

When Willie Kriegslin followed Jaeger Brecht out of the POW camp at Houlton, by less than a half hour, he was, for all his intents, the dumbest of the POWs in the camp. The main thing Willie had in his favor was he knew who Jaeger Brecht was, the Kommando colonel in masquerade, who had completely fooled his American captors into believing he was nothing but another dumb soldier, unaware of the big picture. The Kommando Brecht was the ace up Willie's sleeve.

Brecht had no idea Willie was following him and had generally ignored the comrade who openly admitted, to anyone who was listening, that he was just a dog soldier, a foot slogger only obeying directions of his officers. Back in Edenkoben in the Rhineland, Willie's father was a mere cobbler, struggling in that small town, living veritably from foot to mouth. Willie, at an early age, knew he was destined for the same task; the only other choice was to break out and work in the vineyards. Oftentimes looking at his future, he fostered a joy in hunting and fishing and was comfortable in the forests and in mysterious caves and by the water. All these provided escape for him, never dreaming of being a soldier, until the army pulled him into the ranks. From then on he followed where he was pointed.

Now, at a distance, in all the stealth imaginable, he had followed the Kommando officer, who had carefully planned every step of his escape from the POW camp, through the broken fence, the twisted wires, the open culvert under the last barrier.

All Willie carried with him was a batch of pepper wrapped in a handkerchief and carried in a paper bag. During his potato picking that August, on various farms in the Houlton area, Willie had found the hidden cave at the edge of the Felton place, and had stashed stolen supplies during a month of odd labor, potato picking and daily intrigue… first he placed water in odd containers in the cave, and scrounged food from farmer's wives or daughters, that would last at least a week, perhaps time enough for any concentrated pursuit to slacken. One old map of the state of Maine came into his hands at the back of a barn, and that too rested in the cave.

The pepper was for the dogs that would follow them. He had seen Brecht for weeks take away from meals every bit of pepper he could manage. And Willie followed suit, knowing what the pepper was for. Let the dogs come; all he had to do was to get to the cave, live on his stored supplies, move on later when the pepper did the trick on the dogs, the chase cooled, and the Americans went back to their laid-back ways.

During the escape he dwelled at times on the daughter at the Felton farm who smiled at him once or twice, as if a message was being sent. Emsie was one of prettiest girls he'd seen in America, and she had a good shape, worked hard and was only seventeen. He admired all that in her, and her smile. It was evident to him very early that she turned her back when he was busy at secret things, as if she was eager to help him, or at least averting her eyes; she'd not be a good witness if he fled. With no young men on the farm, Willie was sure he was attractive to her, as she was attracted to him. He began to think about her in that way.

Once, when he went into the barn and stayed there for ten minutes, she had casually walked in and began to talk to him. Willie's English was good enough to be understood, and his leanings for her were clearly pronounced. When she stood close enough for him to kiss her, as if daring him, he did. Her arms wrapped about him and she pressed herself against him. "Willie," she said, "you are the strongest one ever to work here. I like that. I like you, but we have to be careful. My father would beat me if he saw me. He wouldn't understand. He never does."

"You make me dream about you," Willie said, as he hugged her tightly. "I dream about you every night back at the camp. When can I be with you? I do not want you to get into any trouble, because I am meaning to escape from the camp and hide out in the woods. The camp is a horrible place. No privacy. No women, no you, it makes everybody crazy, the way simple things go out of kilter. Things go unbalanced. It happens every day. The men are remembering wives or sweethearts. I have nobody but you to think about. I can be crazy for you, but I don't want you to get in trouble, you work so hard and so good. You work as hard as any man I've ever seen, but you always look better than any of them to me."

There was no argument that she'd be in good hands with Willie Kriegslin. The thought went through her sure as a vow, and as solid. This early in life, she had found her man. Revelations come to the young too, she thought. And she swore she could see the future, could touch it, taste it, bring it to bed with her every night. She hugged him again, in the barn, out of sight of the entire universe itself. She also swore the yellow-green eyes of two horses in separate stalls were looking at her sadly.

In the cave, dark as any night cell and no hope for starlight, Willie imagined what lurked around him. He conjured up a vast array of shapes and shadows in the corners of his eyes.

The odd apparitions of youth came back with their opaque being; he saw things that were not there. Emsie, of course, began her intrusions, three nights in a row assailing him with her trim body, the smell of her skin even in the field under the sun. He would know her any place, could smell her on the thinnest sheet of air. It was the third night, the farm quiet, no stars because of cloud cover, that Willie dared to think about leaving the cave.

The little bag of pepper, which had come in so handy with the dogs in chase, was as good as a weapon. He kept it in a pocket of his pants, and could smell the aroma once in a while. As he was making a decision to at least get some exercise, he heard the first odd noise, first of rock against rock, slight, secretive, then a rustle of clothes, and a small waft of air came against his face and he smelled Emsie, knew she was entering the cave, with the first sound had moved the rock at the entrance.

"Willie," she said, "it's me, Emsie. I'm coming in." Now he could really hear the rustle of her clothes and he caught her scent on a small draft of air, as if she had sent it on to him, to tease him or find acceptance.

"I know you've been hiding here. I'm the only one who knows this place, besides my brother, and he's in California now, working on planes. Even my father doesn't know. He'd skin me alive if he knew I was in here. Would have done it years ago, too. So we never told him. I haven't been in here since my brother Jimmy left. He had to go. My father treated him like a disaster, kept after him forever. Jimmy was never going to be like him. I'm staying, have stayed for my mother or I would have followed Jimmy to the West Coast. I could be making planes that are fighting your army, your friends. I hate war. It's so cruel. We should all be friends, but I'm afraid we can't be friends with Hitler. Even some of your own army officers tried to kill him. Why did they do that?

"Can you stay with me?

"Only until 3 in the morning or about then. He's always up by 5; hard work is all he knows."

"Do you want to stay?"

"That's why I came. I've been dreaming about you. Like every night. I don't think of you as an enemy. I can't explain it all, but I had to come. I knew you were here the first night, but I didn't want you to get caught. There have been soldiers everywhere, even dogs sniffing around, but they didn't come near this cave. They went on past the end of the wall and into the woods at the end of the field."

She was in his arms and her essence assailed him. It was as if she was all exposed with her clothes still on.

"Last warnin', to the pair of ya. Git out'n here now fore I let loose. Emsie, you come first, girl. I ain't meaning' to shoot ya, but I sure am itchin' with this trigger."

"Pa, we're coming together. Don't dare shoot. I'm not letting go of him. I love him, Pa, I don't care if he is a German. He's the man I want to marry some day."

"And let me be the laughin' stock of the whole town. Not on your bottom dollar."

"You use their muscle to get your potatoes, and you'll spend the earnings, but you won't listen to what fits me."

Emsie came out first, as she pulled Willie along behind her coming out of the cave. She stood up shielding Willie, directly in front of the shotgun. "I love him, Pa. Don't make any mistake about that. I've spent near a week with him, right here. Don't spoil anything, Pa."

Her father, taking one hand off the gun, slapped her hard on the face. Willie leaped at him. The shotgun went off and Willie, wounded for the first time since entering the army, screamed in pain. He fell to the ground. Emsie screamed at her father and then pulled the gun out of his hands. He had never shot a man before.

Shouts came from back at the farmhouse and barn. Dogs barked. An engine, loud in the pre-dawn, roared down on them from the service road.

Soldiers came. They put Willie in the back of the truck. Emsie kissed him goodbye as three soldiers laughed at her. "He's the goods, is he? Nothing but a Kraut. Ya ought to know better. They'll take care of him now, probably knock a rape charge against him." The talker, a sergeant, looked at Emsie's father. "How's that sit with you, sir, a rape charge. We'll make it tight. Make it stick. Me and these others practically came right up on them, him, in the act. In a dark cave to boot. Be a piece of cake making it stick. It might be a little easier for you around here, knowing what the neighbors'll make of all this, a loose farm girl you know."

"Go to hell with your rape charge," said Emsie, "and your noise about a loose farm girl. I'll bet you weren't so lucky, not around here anyway. I love him. He's going to be my husband some day when the war is over." For one bare moment, she was an historian looking down the road in front of her. "All wars get over, and friends get made up again. You'll see." She stared at Willie leaning out of the back of the truck. "Willie, I'll love you all the way until this war gets over. You remember where I am. I'll be here. If they try to charge you with rape, I'll go to the newspapers myself, or I'll go down to the camp and make hell for them. You're going to be my husband someday."

"Not going to be no husband, not on my farm, he ain't," her father said.

The sergeant added his own forecast, "We'll ship him so far from here, he'll never find his way back. Does that suit you, sir? That make it up to you for what's happened here?" Emsie remembered the sergeant was the one who had twisted Willie's arm half up his backside when he shoved him into the truck, with pleasure riding his smile, and knew his face would forever be at call. At that moment she also realized that he would share space with Willie in her mind. It reinforced a belief she held that love could often be unfair.

Resolute, a small storm riding her backside, anger making way its entry, Emsie turned her back on the sergeant, and leveled a broadside at her father. "Then, I'll just have to go off like my brother did, driven off to the other side of the country just because he didn't see things the way you did." Her father saw his daughter at that instant as solid as the rocks about them.

She turned to her new friend and lover, hope more alive on her face than ever before, eyes vibrant and reaching, casting a sense of ownership, and yet accompanied by an oath in her words. That's when Elwood Felton saw the second materialization of his wife for the first time in years, when Emsie said, "If I ain't here when you come back, Willie, I'll be in Orinda, California with my brother Jimmy. Jimmy Felton, Orinda, California, so far from here nobody else can get there but you, and nobody else wanted there but you." She nodded at the sergeant, "Let this man make a liar out of the truth and see where it gets him before I get done with all this."

She threw Willie a kiss.

In the pale remnants of early morning she was an upright sign of the new day, and over one shoulder, as if called on for dual announcement, the dawn flash leaped up over a crowned hill and stressed her singularity. Emsie Felton was, without sergeant stripes or parental authority, in charge of the future looming in front of them, and the escaped and recaptured German prisoner of war, staring at her over the tailgate of a six-by army truck, believed he was seeing life already unfolding for him from where it had been sent off by another smaller god of the universe. He had met so few of them.

With eight hundred miles of road under my butt in the last three days, my blood sugar barely holding the line, a couple of old wounds still talking sass to me, whatever else was bugging me besides my errand, fell off the face of the Earth when Disher Menkin's wife Elsie, the new widow, still somewhat of a knockout though she'd collected some flesh under her chin she'd never try to hide, a few other imperfections lost in a surprisingly good figure, hardly ever taciturn at best, said, "Where the hell have you been, Coop, when we needed you most?"

A kick in the ass if you ever had one. And she didn't bat an eyelash, stood there at her doorway as though she was measuring, or sorting out, what other kind of welcome she could generate in my direction, finding her own energy before she could dash mine into some ugly pieces. I'd always known how she'd handle a few things from Disher's outspoken resume of her total attributes.

Of course, he'd always arrive at a final delivery with, "That's some kind of woman I married. Some kind of woman." That probably meant, "I love her nevertheless," or "You can really skip most parts except for the good parts."

I'd made that long drive to bury a good buddy and comrade, Disher Menkin, whom I had not conversed with lucidly and face to face in more than thirty-five years. We'd sized up death before, me and Disher. Me, an old man now, Cooper Bothwaite, feeling the grenade rolling in my gut, road dust a new talcum on my teeth, the continual gray light coming off the hood of the car hurting my eyes, as if a mirror had sat mounted on the dashboard the whole way. This is the way it is every day now, stuff coming in bunches, life a bit of companionable misery or whatever you want to call it.

Normally that kind of jibe Elsie threw at me will knock the hell out of any kind of gathering, but in a funeral home, the body on display like sleep was unbroken from the night before, it's as strident as early morning bugle calls. But I always hated reveille and all the other horn-blowing, for that matter. The only one I liked was *Call to the Colors*. It still gets me, right where it hurts the most. But here's this hard-line new widow giving it to me who's been out of the picture more or less for those long thirty-five years, and her, I know, with a chain saw tearing up her heart and loneliness and doubt hitting her right in the face with the reality of five-card draw.

It's not new. I've been there, and it is an odd lot.

God, even being trim and shapely outside of the neck thing, she looked tough, bags under her eyes, tunnels leaning backwards out of them as if she had been there and back in a hurry, large dark spots on her arms as if they were badges of some sort not to be hidden. I know what those oversize freckles are saying out loud to the whole world. But there's no long sleeve cover-up for Disher Menkin's lady. She was front and center as she had always been, as memory served me. Truth is, she had scared the hell out of Disher right from the start. Thing was, he could not stand fakers. The claptrap of bull-shitters really bothered the man. With Disher you had to be up front, and not piecemeal. No phonies ever made it with him, so the straight-out talking lady from Brunswick, Maine impressed him the first time she opened her mouth: "You know, soldier, your uniform looks like frigging hell. Why didn't you have it pressed?" I think Disher fell in love with her right then. Must have been something, because it went on for more than forty-five years, her speaking her mind, Disher hearing every word.

Whether he believed it all is something else. Even foxhole buddies like we were don't tell all, even when the Grim Reaper sits atop the hole with his dark visage and terrible eyes and the edge of the scythe keen as a new bayonet, the sun's glow sitting on the thinnest edge like a match'd been struck.

"Coop," she said, not at all backing off, as if nothing else had happened in the way of the curt introduction, "this is my daughter MayBelle and her husband Nicholas." I could remember Disher saying, on that old gray bucket going toward Europe in 1943, the Atlantic in its own turmoil, rank odors like real characters aboard every corner and stairwell of the ship, "My first-born, if it's a girl, will be called MayBelle. Was my mother's sister's name, and she drowned in the Amicalola River down in topper Ca'lina looking for frogs when she was a kid."

I swear MayBelle looked a bit like her father, eyes as serious as one can make them, like measurement is always going on, and blue-green as if not sure which way to lead. I measured her at the forty years of age I knew her to be. Her skin was nice, and there was no tiredness coming off her face. The ease of one good child can do that for you, and she had but the one boy.

I bet she was more like her father than her mother. Her husband Nicholas, somewhat uncomfortable in a dark suit, was another case. On one hand there was but a finger and a thumb, and the thumb oversize to begin with. Immediately I wondered about their lovemaking; did he make special use of that odd hand? I had heard other stories of such graceful impairment. A man's gotta do what a man's gotta do. But Nicholas was of good size, perhaps a shade over six feet, a full head of blond hair, dark brown eyes rather at acceptance than measurement. I was pretty sure that he was unaware of all the other people in the room. Something in him, in his handshake, in those dark eyes, said he seriously wanted to talk to me.

A crisp impatience kept touching at his person, like a loose ignition wire working its way to something unusual.

"So, you're Coop!" he said, shaking my hand with that odd hand, the grip almost malevolently hard, like handcuffs in operation, but he released the grip quickly. If I didn't have a thumb to counter its slide, he could have manacled me in a hurry. "I've always wanted to meet you. Knew it would come sometime, but never thought it would be this way. Disher loved you, Coop. I can say that without a bit of reservation. We used to sit down in the cellar in summers, cooling off from the hot sun, sipping on beer he made in a big porcelain crock, like dipping in a well with a ladle, stories falling by the wayside on occasion. Those were good times. I think he liked them too, as much as me."

The smile on his face was a full and bright smile loaded with memory. I decided, on the spot, I trusted him. The ladies looked surprised at the quick revelations he spun off. I truly believed he had not spoken of such things with them, had not shared Disher with them, at least not that way, but he could readily share with me.

"He said I'd get to see you sometime if you were still alive, Coop. I guess he was thinking about this." Around the room he looked, a long while at Disher's face over the edge of the casket, then shrugged his shoulders.

"He was positive that I'd meet you. I guess what he was saying is that he knew you'd be here if this happened." He went through the survey with his eyes again. Not once did he look at his wife or his mother-in-law but kept his eyes on mine. I knew he had something else to say; it was there, just off the edge of his voice, behind a small screen in his eyes. His mouth seemed to hold back other words. I felt the impatience again, the distraction of it almost electrical.

Disher's widow said, "Why didn't you come earlier, Cooper? He was ranting and raving at the end. Said your name a hundred times. I sure thought you'd be here earlier. Your buddy, huh?" Pure iron-plate caustic with a phony question mark.

When MayBelle put her hand on her mother's arm, to hold her back a mite, her mother continued, "Disher must have been hiding something all the time. Never once ever said anything to me about a fire, or kids. Never once. But I thank you for making the long trip. They don't get any easier."

Even with that the edge was ax-sharp in her voice. MayBelle jumped in again. "I'm sure Nicholas would like to talk to you away from all this." She took her mother by the arm and was about to lead her toward a couple that had just come into the viewing room. With that move I knew she was Disher's daughter.

Disher's widow Elsie said, "I tried to call you for the last four days. There was no answer. Why don't you have an answering machine? Everybody has one of those contraptions these days. How did you find out about Disher?"

I said, "They called me from the vet's hospital."

"How'd they get your number?" There was a jiggle to the flesh under her chin, and her head was cocked at an angle, the measuring mode still in place.

"I gave it to them four or five weeks ago when I was there to see him."

The bare bones of surprise came up lightly on her face. "He didn't tell me.

Why didn't you call me?"

"He couldn't tell anybody anything. And I came to see Disher, not to socialize." It was a slice of her own cake and she ate it easily. We had made a small peace, if that's what it can be called. I knew that I had been between her and Disher forever. It's like that sometimes, but we never exploited it.

Nicholas, that large thumb hooked onto his pants pocket and partially hidden, and the single finger sitting like a curse along the edge of his pocket, though somewhat undisturbed by any of it, walked me to an anteroom. It was quite evident that he wanted to talk out of earshot of the two women, that he had broached the possibility in front of them and it seemed he had depended on his wife to carry off his subtle need. Her response was, I thought, expected.

Nicholas' shoulders were a good span, his head shapely in an angular and regal manner and the blond head near full of curly tresses cresting the back of his neck. Though there was no other hippie look about him; no beard, no mustache, no heavy growth over the ears, a bit of the rebel mark sat on him, sort of an invisible tattoo. I was not sure if it was the hand that made him different or his locks. With faint stripes that may have been a tint of orange, the dark suit he wore fit him well, saying he was somewhat comfortable in such dress, but not fully at ease. I'd bet he'd get out of it quickly when this occasion was finished.

The anteroom's *No Smoking* sign was small and almost unobtrusively noticeable, the law now a matter of fact, and three elderly gents, sure to be older than my 78 years, had gathered their almost three centuries of experience in a small huddle. It appeared as if they did much of their talking with their hands, their eyes, the almost casual shrug of a shoulder. They could have been marionettes. It reminded me of the ward in the vet's hospital where I last saw my buddy Disher breathing, rolling his eyes at some unknown and past sight, mumbles buried and barreled deep in his throat. I remember thinking then that if this was down the road for me, I'd make sure the road had a bridge that was washed out and I'd drive like hell heading for it.

With that solitary and awful finger, showing an ordinary use, Nicholas pointed to two big easy chairs sitting in a far corner of the second anteroom. "Those ought to do us." Over his shoulder he looked and said, "There are times when I have to stay out of earshot of that woman. She does take aim when she wants. Never bothered Disher, that I know of."

I just had to ask. "What was all that about back there, other than Elsie being her curt self? She hasn't changed a bit though I haven't seen her practically since ever. You and MayBelle must keep a good chunk of Disher handy."

Nicholas had made himself comfortable in one of the chairs, though sitting near the edge, and he let the awful hand sit in his lap like a bone remnant on an empty plate. Looking at me, his eyes were locked on a sadness I could only guess at. His blond eyebrows, close to a gray snow left over from plowing, aged him slightly but with a kindness. He would have been, I assessed quickly, a welcome companion, a comrade, dependable, durable, on for the long ride wherever it went, Grim Reaper and all.

"I wanted to talk to you about that," Nicholas said. "It's been bugging me. Hell, it's been bugging Elsie like a burr under her bonnet. I guess she suspects that whatever was going on with Disher at the end, down there at the vet's hospital where they took such damned good care of him, like a baby I swear, you somehow have privy to and she doesn't. It was not something he was letting go of, perhaps repressed and trying to come out of him at the end. And it looks like she can't let go of it either, her not knowing. She's one tough woman, fair as hell, but tough. The shot's there to be fired, take it; or take the one coming back at you."

"You mean Disher was talking at the end? I was with him for four hours one day, just weeks ago, and he never uttered a sound. He looked at me a few times, like he knew who I was. I suspect he did, his eyes settling on me an old look, a glance of sorts I might have seen before in him, but never said my name once, nor anybody's name. None of the old outfit. Not a one."

I twisted around in the chair as Nicholas' awful hand settled in his good hand, peace settling down in place like ashes. "What happened? What did Disher say thats got to Elsie so hard?" I wanted to ask if it was the French girl he had spent the night with in an old farmhouse one Christmas Eve. It hung on him for a long while afterward, but I kept it all back where it belonged, in the past.

Nicholas looked over his shoulder, back at the viewing room, and the ladies out of sight, the first nervous strain he'd shown to me, a new side of him under some import I am sure. "He was kind of noisy at the end, old Disher, the last couple of weeks, on the downhill run if you want to know, getting so thin, like he was melting away. I'd swear to God his face was like the side of a cereal box, pushed in, his dentures big as lumps in his face, oversize like. Lots of crying, calling out some strange names, ones I'd never heard, then kept crying more and yelling out, The babies! The babies! He did that loudest. I mean, that's when he got real loud, and then wailed like a lost kid himself, shaking in the bed. Jeezus, his arms were going crazy, his legs kicking, his head jerking around like he's looking for somebody or something. We had to tie him in a few times, get restraints from the ward nurse. I don't mind telling you, Coop, he scared the hell out of me."

Again, he looked back at the other room. "I know some of the names were French girls' names, at least they sounded that way to me. Elsie never heard or never said anything. I figured she didn't hear or recognize them because, knowing her, she sure would have had a few things to say about it. Wouldn't be like her to let something like that get by her, I don't care how long ago it was."

At first nothing came to me, as if a silence had been etched, a darkness convened. Being notoriously drunk for some period of your life locks away lots of memories. For a drunken rifleman, a footslogger, soldier of the earth, being a stranger in a strange land, loss of some kind is guaranteed. So, it was not surprising that nothing immediately in that anteroom, near the visible death of my old comrade and fellow warrior, his widow's tongue tart and afoot, made a connection for me; not Nicholas, not any picture on the walls, not the ladies in the other room whose voices were barely audible in turning that corner between us.

To me there is such a thing as horizon-peeking, a cyclical break in the clouds, an opening. Perhaps it's a light down a narrow tunnel or through an old casement window of sorts, and, at best, ephemeral. Slowly but surely the face of a French girl came to me, pale but pretty, eyes set up with a haunting deep as caves, the half globes of her cheeks tarnished by something I could not read other than war. Perhaps, I surmised, she came out of a cloud, certainly she was cloud-like, just as if she was lit up, neon-ed, her face in a sunny glow, the softness of her lips her sole and most animate prize.

She had spent the night in a barn with Disher, a barn leaning every which way to ruin; the doors missing so that you could see out the back end, but not see the stalls or the haymow, or where the dusk coming in took them. They were like kids in love for one night.

Next morning a German .88 took her and a kid brother at the well. She was standing there in a blue dress with the ladle in her hand, leaning against the rock wall like sex personified and perfected, the thrust of her stomach arched and tormenting, the little brother waiting to take his turn, and *wham*! they're gone. Just like that! I heard the stuff coming in but didn't even have time to duck. You couldn't pick them up with a blotter, neither one of them. Of course, I'd been on that royal drunk and didn't know how much it hit Disher until later. But we were all screwed up. We'd pillaged a small village. Brandy and cognac were like water around us, coming up out of cellars and dim recesses and who knows where else. Some was given to us, some was taken, retribution for time spent, wounds received, hell paying out its dues. I drank the stuff like I drink beer sometimes, guzzling it. Lord, I could have washed in it. I was thinking that a whole bunch of some of those days had passed me by, lost for years.

Now here's my buddy, gone from me, gone from all of us, bringing me back, waking me up. I can smell the day, the village, the liquor, the hay, the barn, the smoke, can see them at the well and then gone from the well. In the back of my head, at some point where it seemed I had been raking the compost of that mind, scenes and images are breaking down, coming apart, falling out of the darkness like a pile of dominoes being spilled. Pictures. Pictures. Pictures.

Then it came. Over the long years it came. Over half a century of my life, through darkness and uncertainty, through turmoil, and this newest death, it came. And there was another barn and a German trooper, half dressed, we'd cut down in a small farmyard, a hail of bullets going in there, raking him, a gray tunic in one hand and his rifle in the other, not quite ready for the rest of the war. I saw smoke, and the barn is burning and tossing off clouds of black smoke and a woman's screaming and we see her at the haymow window. She's holding a baby. There's another kid at her elbows, standing right beside her. Disher runs up to the barn. 'Throw the baby down! Throw the baby down!' he yells. She doesn't know what to do I guess, Disher probably no different from the German we'd just shot, the one not dressed all the way like he'd been taking his own liberties. Then Disher says, back over his shoulder, after trying to get the door open, "There's a lock on the door. The Kraut locked her in!" Disher doesn't use his rifle to shoot the lock off. He runs back to get an ax or something from the farmhouse porch and a Six-by drives into the yard. Disher jumps up in the seat and pushes the driver over. I heard him yell, 'There's kids in there.' He drives the Six-by over to the barn and points to the canvas top. 'Throw the baby down,' he says and makes gestures to the mother.

She throws the baby down and it lands on the canvas top. Christ, it almost bounced off the canvas, the baby. Another GI grabs the kid. Disher yells at her again. 'Throw the other one down.' She doesn't move. He backs the truck up and rams the locked door. The building shakes and the woman disappears. Puff she's gone! And the other kid disappears and the roof comes down on the whole goddamn barn. Flames come shooting like only dust is burning, or gases. Lots of it. Like acetylene. Like a frigging torch and Disher goes batty. Loses it, he does. The whole thing. Thinks he knocked her deeper into the fire, was the cause of her death, who knows how many kids might have been in there.

You think I'd been drunk on that toot, man? You ought to see Disher after that, fucking hoot-owl drunk for nearly three days, and we kept moving and I kept him out of the limelight and out of serious trouble. Pulled a detail or two for him. When he woke up one morning, rank but sober, he never mentioned it again. Hell, I had forgotten it too. But it looks like Disher never let go of it, him being with that other girl too, like he had been punished for the little fun he had. Like he worried about Elsie coming at him the way she can, all mouth and hellfire, and I swear the end of the world in it. But he loved her. Old Disher never let go of that either. He loved her right to the bitter end."

I had to lay off Nicholas after that, so much coming at him all at once, and the voices rising in the other room, as if they were on the way to invade our privacy. I looked at Nick and said, trying to poke it all together for him, "They're going to say in the funeral service that he'll soon be in the company of angels. I knew him in the company of men. And he was the best of them, old Disher was."

"There they are, locked up in some more damn secrets I'll bet." I didn't even have to look up to see who was talking. And Disher was probably totally deaf by then.

Connaughton's Reflex

For years Connaughton believed his bakery window lied to him. The name Sligo Bakery spread its gold letters all across the huge plate glass of his shop near the great church. For twenty-seven years, with the pies and tarts and breads and cakes all about him, he held to this belief. Though rock-ribbed in a stoic rhythm, he alluded the lies might have been caused by reflections from morning or evening sun, a streetlight at a surmising or refracting angle, a pair of headlights bouncing from a late taxi or a loud truck out on the avenue of industry. Light and shadows, the way he carried an argument, were always in a kind of partnership.

Constantly reaching for answers, he kept hoping for some trust and resolution from the pane of glass. He found it more than intriguing that any time he was at the pie table in the back end of the bakery or stacking loaves and looking out at the front window, the window was lying to him, presenting a side of life not quite with it. That life, he often thought, grasping for blame, surmising why it was always him coming out on the hard side, had lied from the very beginning, had twisted everything. His wife, though a good wife and a hard-working one, was consigned for years now to her wheelchair; his dreams were thus in permanent partition. Mostly he was an honest man, though he felt his manhood was spoiled by a deadly blow performed out and beyond his ken. Where he practiced a deep celibacy from a conviction rising from a deeper trust, nothing at times came up real.

And the window scenes were mostly small intrusions in his busy life, episodes, pauses and recreations of nobler life, as if he had neither the time nor the interest in seeing their vapid conclusions, if indeed there were any conclusions. Damned reflections, were they not? He was a baker, was he not? Bread, the bread of life as it were, could not wait, the hot loaf a special commodity to local folk who bought, bargained, sometimes pleaded with him for a few slices. Connaughton always gave in; he hated hunger, stories from the old land still packed their intrusive ways deep in his memory box, coming from the dank rooms of his childhood.

This day, at the outset, promised to have no exceptions from the usual.

He told his wife Gertrude, industriously working from her wheelchair, "You won't believe what I saw today." He nodded his head in a slight affirmation. "Just this morning." For the seeming thousandth time she raised her eyebrows and her head, according to the expression on Connaughton's face, knowing that his "today" meant "just now," his "just this morning" meant when she had turned her head away from the window for a split second.

Though she loved him from their first dance in grade school, had loved his thick mop of dark hair and his wide smile, he'd always had a way with imagination. She had no idea he thought his view of himself was like looking in a faulty age mirror, the kind that tells one's image that it's younger than it is, and the other much older. Gertrude, in her special chair, at crust and crullers, powder gracing her in a small way, every morning her hair whiter than ordinary with the reach of the flour, was an invalid, and had not been out of her apartment without her husband for too many years to count. She came to the bakery with him in the pre-dawn, went home at lunchtime by his hand, to wait for his evening arrival. The evening stories were often very special, though she believed he created them to give her life a dash of salt. Some of them were so salty they made her roar with laughter, or brought tears to her eyes.

He pleased her; she pleased him.

"Some men robbed the bank across the street. They were running out and O'Malley yelled at them when he came around the corner and pulled his gun." He announced his next statement like a news anchor on the television news broadcast. "They shot Officer O'Malley on the spot." Connaughton's face was red in disbelief of what he believed.

"Shot him dead on the spot! I saw it with my own eyes." He shook his head again, the way he had a hundred or more other times.

"What movie did you watch last night?" Gertrude said. "Is there something yet stuck on the back of your eyeball, part of the movie you liked least but remember most?"

Gertrude smiled when O'Malley slipped in the door a half hour later for his morning coffee and two slices of warm bread thick with butter. He waved to her in the back room when the swinging door swung open. "Still at it, Gertie? Don't you get tired supporting that old geezer?" His belly rolled its blue wave, his eyes shone in admiration. He waved goodbye, nodding at the same time his respects as Gertrude said, "You say hi to Grace for me."

Later in the day, just before lunch break, the window caught Connaughton's eye again, the lie full and colorful, as real as he could make it. Molly O'Hara from a flat on the third floor of the opposite corner, so early in the day in her evening attire, peered into the bakery. One hand shielded her eyes, deep and dark. Though she was but thirty, she looked fifty; life on the street and a child back at the flat having worked their ways on her. Often a loaf of Connaughton's bread was all that came between her and outright hunger.

Connaughton wanted to say something to Gertrude, but she was icing a cake at last, the end of her morning run. She was intent at her task, the best icer he ever had.

Words rose up out of Connaughton as if they had been strained; "Will you look who's hungry now, Gertie. Molly's been sick a few days and most likely needs some bread. I'll go tend her." The rouged face appeared lit like a neon. The cheeks of the night were cardinal red, scandal red, breathing red. The thin silk dress barely covered Molly's prominent breasts, their nipples like pin pricks pointing at him. He remembered the night a dozen years earlier he had found himself in her room, had shaken himself from hunger, left abruptly never to go back. That was not an illusion; had never been an illusion. Her small room had ached with a smell of sweet wine. There were times he had great difficulty removing the scent from his thoughts.

Then, in the newest reflection, in a piece of shattered light, he saw a big man grab Molly's slim arm, shake her and grab her slight pocketbook. Any man should have known the slim bag, carried loosely on her shoulder, was empty. Connaughton turned his head, disbelief and belief rushing into the fray together, pulling at him. Some days he could have screamed but Gertrude could not help him with the stuff he could never admit. When he looked back Molly O'Hara was closing the door behind her, flashing green dollars over her head. "What I owe you, sweet Paulie. Just what I owe you. Met a feller last night wants to take care of me and little Michael for good. This one's real!" The evening face had a morning brightness.

She smiled at him, shrugged a shoulder so that Gertrude could not see, and said, "I'll have two hot loaves while we're at it." The look on her face told him the story about the new feller could be real. He'd pray for it later.

Later that day the skies turned a different shade of gray, full of wrath and promise, darker than they had been for months, and swirling snow came with the grayness. Connaughton saw two shadows in his window, one he had seen before, a day earlier, a young boy and he had been told the boy's name was John. He was twelve years old and a street person. The clothes the boy wore told the story. They were old and worn and torn, and dirty looking. One pocket of his thin jacket was missing. His pants were short. His socks did not match. He had no hat on his head. His hair was very dark and he was standing in front of the Sligo Bakery near the big cathedral. A tall man in worn clothes was standing with him, and they were looking at food in the bakery window. Around them swirled the cold wind and the snow of a sudden storm on a late December evening.

Connaughton looked out the window at them. A strange glow was fuzzy around the boy's head. Connaughton was drawn to him. He had been pulled from the back of the bakery when he saw the boy standing at the window looking so hungry. In Connaughton's blood raced a new sensation. He could feel it coursing. It was the same feeling he had when the anthem was played. When he heard a beautiful psalm it came to him, or when a far and lovely voice at nightfall sang an old song he had nearly forgotten, the special way it came out of the past bringing all kinds of delightful company with it, like a Percy French song echoing from the Cliffs of Mohr. Oh, he thought, the deliriums of joy.

Connaughton waved them into the shop, in from the cold and the swirling snow. The tall man shook his head and pointed to the boy. Even in his shabby clothes the man bore to Connaughton a sense of regality and pride, yet he had a kindly presence about him. The man refused a second invitation and again pointed to the boy. As bidden the boy entered the bakery and Connaughton put six rolls and a cup of coffee in a bag. The boy looked back at the man standing outside the window.

"My father says you are a good man," the boy said to Connaughton, "but he's not hungry right now." The baker and the boy turned and the man was gone. The boy ran outside and the man was gone. The snow was worsening and it was colder. The boy cried, "My father has left me. My father has gone." He looked at Connaughton and said again, in the saddest voice Connaughton had ever heard, "My father has left me."

Connaughton did not know what to do. His job he could not leave, and there was no place to take the boy. Then he saw a street person he recognized, a good man by the name of Samuel Haggard. He called him over to the bakery.

"Samuel," he said, "this boy's name is John and his father has left him. I'm afraid of what will happen to him in the night. Can you take care of him?"

Samuel looked at the boy John and saw the golden light that was like a faint glow around the boy's head. When he put his hand on the boy's shoulder he was warmed by the touch. "I know a place where he can sleep," he said. It's only a closet, but there's lots of paper and cardboard and he will not freeze."

Connaughton gave them more rolls and coffee and went back to work. Only when he was inside did he realize that he had not been cold at all when he had gone outside in the bitter night to talk to Samuel. He waved at the boy John and Samuel as they walked off into the darkness.

As they walked Samuel said he was sorry that the boy's father was gone.

The boy John said, "Do not feel sorry for me, Samuel. My father loves me. Some time he will come back for me." The golden glow was stronger around the boy's head.

Other street people that knew Samuel came up to him as they walked. "Who is this boy, Samuel?" they said. They stared at the boy John. Many street people stared and asked the same question. Many of them had seen the glow around the boy's head, though some had not seen it. They did not know what to make of their old friend Samuel and the strange new boy who looked so much like they did. His clothes were like their clothes. He looked as lonely as they looked. He had no real place of his own to go to on a cold December night, no real place to put down his head for the night; no fire, no blanket, no cradling arms.

Samuel said to the boy John, "Would you like to go to the cathedral to warm up before we go to a place to sleep?"

The boy John said, "Don't you go to the cathedral to pray, Samuel?" The glow was more golden and brighter and made Samuel uneasy, not sure of what it was. He just knew that here was something different around the boy and around his own person.

In the cathedral a crowd of street people had gathered. Word had spread quickly in the alleys and the lanes and the byways about the boy with a golden ring about his head. Most of the people agreed it was a ring. Not one of them had called it a halo.

In the subway stations, also, people spoke about him. Word spread up and down the Green Line and the Red Line and the Orange Line. On the back sides of chimneys, and tight against warm walls, and on warm exhaust grates, the street people talked about the boy. There was a buzz and a hum about him. The word carried far and wide. It rippled and ran with the wind.

The people who came to the cathedral at first were seedy looking. Their clothes were in tatters. Some of them wore rolls of cloth around their feet and about their waists. Some wore old sneakers or thin worn shoes. Few of them had good jackets or coats or scarves or warm gloves for their tortured hands. They came to look at the boy with a golden ring about his head and who had no place to go to call his own, the boy who was so much like them.

The next night Samuel took the boy John back to the cathedral. Now hundreds of people were there. Some of them laughed and scoffed and said they could not see any light at all, never mind a golden ring. Many new arrivals wore nice clothes and heavy coats and thickly padded jackets against the cold. High boots many of them wore and scarves and great warm gloves on their hands. Indeed, some of them did not laugh for they believed they saw the golden light.

Samuel brought the boy John back to the cathedral each night. It was getting close to Christmas and the crowds grew and the bishop called for police help with the crowds along the cluttered streets. All kinds of people from all over were coming to the cathedral to see the boy. You could tell by the clothes they wore, or what kind of vehicle brought them to the great church.

Samuel warmed up in the cathedral each time and the boy John prayed for his father to come back. He kept telling Samuel that his father loved him and would come back for him. Samuel did not know what to believe. He just knew he had to bring the boy back each night in spite of the crowd's gawking at him. The snickers and the scoffing bothered Samuel. At times he grew impatient with people he knew for a long time.

"He's just a boy whose father left him," explained Samuel as often as he could. But he did not believe what he was saying. The light was getting too bright for him to handle. He asked a friend to bring the boy John to the cathedral the next night. It would be Christmas Eve.

All day the snow fell. The temperature also fell with the late hours. The darker it got, the colder it got.

But a greater crowd than ever before came on Christmas Eve. They packed the old cathedral. Every seat was taken. The aisles were full. People stood all around looking at the boy John down in the front row. Some saw the light. Some did not. But none of them left the cathedral then. Some were afraid to go. Some, indeed, were afraid to stay.

The bishop, at the back of the altar, tried desperately to see the golden glow. He was not sure what he was seeing. A young priest from a nearly forgotten order saw the golden ring around the boy's head. Clearly he saw it. He spoke to the bishop for a few minutes and came to the front of the congregation.

"We know why some of us have come here tonight. Some have come for the right reason. Some have not. It may be that some will be rewarded and some will not. And that may be as it was meant to be. I will ask the boy John to come up here and talk to us if he feels like it."

He extended his open hand to the boy John.

The boy John went to the front of the altar. "I am very nervous," he said.

"Do not be nervous," the young priest replied. "We are all sorry that your father has left you."

"Do not be sorry for me. I love my father very much," the boy John said, "and he loves me. Some time he will come back to get me."

"Do you want to tell us anything?" the young priest said. He looked directly at the boy John and did not look at the bishop at the back of the altar.

"One night, at a campfire on a cold night, my father took off his coat and gave it to a man who did not have a coat. He said, 'Now we will both be warm.'"

The young priest did not say anything. The bishop did not say anything. The boy John looked at the huge gathering. No one in the congregation said anything. No one did anything. The huge cathedral was silent, silent in the nave, silent in the apse, and silent in the transept. You could not hear people breathe or cough or blow their noses as you did at other times. Their feet also were still and silent on the floor.

The boy John with the golden glow around his head said, "That's the beautiful picture I have. It's the most beautiful picture of all. That each person who has a coat or a heavy jacket would give it to a person who does not have a warm coat or a heavy jacket. Or give a warm hat to someone who has no hat or a scarf to someone who has no scarf or a great pair of gloves to someone whose hands might freeze before this night is over. My father says you will be warmer, and my father loves me very much, and I love my father even though he has gone from me for this while."

Again, for long minutes, there was silence in the great cathedral. Nothing moved. No one moved. Stillness was sharp as the cold. It was only the wind that was heard, from the belfry and at the windows as if it were trying to get inside. The boy John looked at the congregation. Now, as if predicted, more people began to see the glow that they had not seen before. Inside them things were working they had no control over. Then, in the midst of the great silence, one man in the fifth row, in a fine and heavy coat, thick and furry, stood up and took the coat off his shoulders and handed it to a man sitting in front of him. That man had no coat but wore a thin and worn sweater atop another thin and worn sweater. No words were exchanged.

Then another man stood in the silence and gave his coat. And another. And another. And a pair of great fleece-lined gloves moved from one pair of hands to another, and a scarf, and more and more, until the sounds of giving swelled throughout the whole insides of the cathedral as if a soft wind was blowing.

And the boy John smiled at all the people and at the young priest and at the bishop. Then he said, loud enough for everybody in the cathedral to hear, "I do not want anyone who gave his coat or hat or gloves to another person to get cold tonight going home. If there is a taxicab driver who can help get those people home, everyone will be warmer."

In the back row a man stood up and said, "I have my cab and I'll call my friends who have cabs."

When the people left the cathedral a short time later there were many cabs in the street, their lights glowing golden through the edge of darkness. It looked like a parade of taxicabs.

And Samuel Haggard, coming late to the cathedral, saw in the distance, in the swirling snow, in the region past the crowd, the boy John walking off into the endless night with his hand in his father's hand.

And the glow over his head had faded away.

Speak of Relocation

It was July of 1936, sticky hot, perhaps ice cream someplace I hoped, but I was acutely aware that ice cream might not happen this day. The steel bars of Boston's old Mystic Bridge in my hands were hard and warm, as the sun had hours of penetration and I had one hour to spare within my dramatic playground out over the Mystic River we called "The Oily" with observant regard for its rainbowed surface. Having slipped inside the girder work of a cage-like support angled at 45 degrees, my eyes went directly down on a boat about to pass under the bridge loaded with iron junk, old cold steel, surely lots of brass and copper from junk yards and junk wagons all over the city and local areas. Long lengths of copper and brass, gleaming in the mess, looked like sandwich parts between dark iron crusts. The bridge sat between Boston's Charlestown borough, proud as the Bunker Hill Monument, off across the borough and uphill from me, and Chelsea, a city as small in area as one can imagine, but lined with petrol tanks and ship piers, ships that traveled the high seas from countries around the globe ... *the coming-from and the going-to so different.*

I wondered where this ship was going, why junk was the cargo, all that clap-trap debris of the deserted, from wayside conglomerations and ruins and cast-offs that old men in thick white whiskers and beards picked up in horse-drawn wagons and now and then a small red truck with high red sideboards, a step up from the horse vehicle, for delivery and sale at junkyards in the area. The answers came later, in one fell swoop of destiny. There was a singular difference in the cargo of outgoing ships and the junk wagons; the ships only carried metal while the junk wagons also carried scrap paper and cardboard baled tight with rope or wire or old neckties whose patterns still showed off their styles, and bales of old rags in new patterns.

That July of 1936 saw me on vacation from Miss Finn's first grade class at the Kent School, not far from Hobie's Beanery, in a garage of all places, nor far Abie's Market on one strategic corner of the Loop-the-Loop, and the Bond Bread factory. All of them memorable for one or more reasons, and I still have the note Miss Finn sent home to my parents: "Please don't move away until I have taught all the Sheehans." Miss Finn thought my sister Patricia and I were her bright stars; we were readers at this early age, taken in hand by a paternal grandmother and a paternal grandfather for the grasp of one of "the three Rs." (We had no idea, my sister Pat and I, that we were bound for Marleah Graves' second grade class at the Cliftondale School in Saugus, only a dozen miles away, and a host of new classmates bound to be SHS '47.)

And yet here I was adventuring within the structure of a monster bridge, a structure that continually enticed me with solid come-ons. Once, a few months earlier, I had traversed over the river's water as the bridge opened to let a ship pass under its span. That one-time terror became, for a free lancer kid, a constant challenge to do it again, to out-do my first fear, to be, as my father used to say, "One of the survivors of the times that flag about us." I knew what he was referring to ... always hungry for the thin meals that came from nowhere into my mother's hands in our third level kitchen on Bunker Hill Avenue; some of those Depression-era meals so immemorial they are most memorable the longer I hold onto them. Let's say about 87 years now, stretching on, keeping cover. An instance would be a Sunday meal purchased for a dollar after church: at Hobie's Beanery a quart of baked beans and a loaf of brown bread and the balance spent in Abie's Market, closed on Sunday but entered via the back door for all the lamb kidneys I could get from Abie. Abie favored us too, for my sister once told him, "You grow the best lamb kidneys of all, but they still stink up the house when they're getting cooked." He loved her honesty and winked his appreciation for me, and I couldn't wait to tell my parents; *good news was always in order.*

If my father knew I was in that cage-like support, he'd whale the tar out of me; my mother would cast a stern look, shake her head, begin to cry at the possibilities. But ... and a big imaginative BUT, my grandmother, likely on that same July day, put on her pert little black hat, grabbed her black shiny pocketbook and took the first bus that came by her corner of Highland Avenue and Trull Lane in Somerville, a few miles away, the tall, elegant lady of manners, most correct speech, possibly the softest hands I've ever known, and words that often said, *"We are born to read."*

More than three-quarters of her life were spent binding books at Ginn & Company in Cambridge, with hundreds of rejects landing on our shelves from inside her shiny black pocketbook, those very books calling out, making demands, crying for attention to favored paragraphs beginning the longest lingering that bunches of words ever had. (The High Lama saying in *Lost Horizon,* *"For when that day comes, the world must begin to look for a new life. And it is our hope that they may find it here. For here, we shall be with their books and their music, and a way of life based on one simple rule: Be Kind! When that day comes, it is our hope that the brotherly love of Shangri-La will spread throughout the world. Yes, my son; When the strong have devoured each other, the Christian ethic may at last be fulfilled and the meek shall inherit the earth."*)

She was, on that day or one just like it, bent on travel and transportation and relocation ... of our family. "Find some grass and trees for the boy, friends for the girls, room to breathe, throw arms and yells into the sky, climb the hills, fish the ponds, let them be." A hundred times I had heard her say to my father, "Let them be, James. Let them be," That *BE* was stretched as far as she could send it. Too much too soon she had seen more than once; in our own doorway the drunk of early morning advertising his hard, harsh night, half alive, meaning half dead, sprawled in his helplessness, his loss, extravagance afoot gone prone, a disastrous sight for an elegant grandmother, bookbinder, dreamer, mover of families. There was a better place. Perhaps she had paused as I had on that same elocution of the High Lama, where each of us had seen Hugh Conway nod his head in universal agreement, in solitude's assessment. Some grandmothers are like that; *lucky us.*

That grand day of decision, she went via Somerville/Everett Station/Malden Square to find a big silver Hart Lines bus that simply said "Saugus" on its destination sign. She found a third floor apartment in Cliftondale Square beside Hanson's Garage, near Joe Laura's Barbershop and Louie Gordon's Tailor Shop, and gave acute directions to my father ... *take them elsewhere.* That's how we were bound for Saugus, where the green grass grew, huge fields of it.

We had, of course, moved before ... several moves ahead of unpaid landlords, in the midst of Prohibition and the Great Depression, and my father's pay of $28.00 a month as a Marine. We weren't taught frugality; we learned it first-hand.

Ahead of the moving van, he took me for my first ride to Saugus. We crossed "my bridge" on the way. Eventually we went along the river and a small fleet of lobster boats (I mentioned that I'd never had lobster and my father said, "Don't worry anymore," as he tousled my hair), cruised through the awed parts of town full of green grass in exorbitant spreads, lusty farms teeming with crops taller than me, rode the Turnpike that headed all the way to Newburyport ... and beyond? I heard the hum of traffic in prolonged sprints rather than the in-town screeches of a daring rider performing a Loop-the-Loop, tire cries as high-pitched as police whistles. Then we circled around until we had seen the three ice houses along the banks of Lily Pond and huge fish, which were carp, roiling in wide circles on the surface and kids jumping off a rocky place into the pond. A few older folks, on the far side, were almost in the darkness of trees as thick as parade crowds, swinging their fishing lines out over the pond where the leaning sun leaped westward back across the Turnpike. And one canoeist, motionless, most distant but ever since a part of this history, dazzled in the sun's rays, such a far cry from the drunk in the doorway who startled and started my grandmother on her own crusade, her own trek here ... *a journey for family preservation.*

I was locked into Saugus already, the images flying through me from the river and the pond and a small, decrepit building with high black letters on its gray side that almost squawked out "Shadowland."

"It used to be a ballroom," my father said, qualifying my curiosity. "Looks like it's gone into the Nevernever land."

But I could tell he was up to something, something special, something to fit, "Find some grass and trees for the boys." It was the male connection. It would not be a place where he'd say to the girls, "This is where you'll play with your dolls, or practice early make-up treats, wear dresses and gowns and high heels that are too many years bigger than you."

We spun a quick left hand turn and a broad field swept out in front of me, with uniform chalk lines at uniform distances, a gridiron. Then and still now, longer than I could run ahead of others, a baseball diamond in one corner backstopped by a huge tree looking surely able to trap foul balls in its thick spread.

In the air was a hush, minutes long, a declaration, a testament. He waited while the images came and went, then simply added, "This'll be for your brother and you. The girls will find their own places. They always will.

About the Author

Thomas F. Sheehan served in the 31st Infantry, Korea, 1951-52, and graduated Boston College, 1956. Books include *Epic Cures*; *Brief Cases, Short Spans*; *The Saugus Book*; *This Rare Earth & Other Flights*; *Ah, Devon Unbowed*; *Reflections from Vinegar Hill*. eBooks include *Korean Echoes* (nominated for a Distinguished Military Award), *The Westering*, (nominated for National Book Award); from *Danse Macabre* are *Murder at the Forum, Death of a Lottery Foe, Death by Punishment, An Accountable Death* and *Vigilantes East. A Collection of Friends, From the Quickening, In the Garden of Long Shadows, The Nations, Where Skies Grow Wide, Cross Trails, The Cowboys, Between Mountain and River, Catch a Wagon to the Stars*, and *Beside the Broken Trail* were published by Pocol Press, and *Six Guns, Inc.*, by Nazar Look, in Romania. Sheehan has multiple works at these sites: *Rosebud, Linnet's Wings, Serving House Journal, Copperfield Review, KYSO Flash, La Joie Magazine, Soundings East, Literary Orphans, Indiana Voices Journal, Frontier Tales, Western Online Magazine, Provo Canyon Review, Nazar Look, Eastlit, Rope & Wire Magazine, Ocean Magazine, The Literary Yard, Green Silk Journal, Fiction on the Web, The Path, Faith-Hope and Fiction, The Cenacle*, etc. Sheehan's tales have produced 30 Pushcart nominations, and five Best of the Net nominations (and one winner) and short story awards from Nazar Look for 2012-2015. *Swan River Daisy* was recently released by *KY Stories* and *Back Home in Saugus*, 200 pages, 90,000 words, and a chapbook, *Small Victories for the Soul*, are on proposal. (His Amazon Author's Page, Tom Sheehan – is on the Amazon site.)